Robert and
Dawn Marie
4ever

Robert and Dawn Marie 4ever

by Miriam Cohen

1 8 1 7

HARPER & ROW, PUBLISHERS

Cambridge, Philadelphia, San Francisco, London, Mexico City, São Paolo, Singapore, Sydney

NEW YORK

Robert and Dawn Marie 4ever
Copyright © 1986 by Miriam Cohen

Designed by Joyce Hopkins

1 2 3 4 5 6 7 8 9 10
First Edition

Library of Congress Cataloging-in-Publication Data
Cohen, Miriam.
　　Robert and Dawn Marie 4ever.

　　Summary: A fourteen-year-old boy in Brooklyn who
has grown up in the foster care system discovers
respect and love with a parochial school girl and with
the eccentric couple who take him in.
　　[1. Brooklyn (New York, N.Y.)—Fiction.
2. Foster home care—Fiction] I. Title. II. Title:
Robert and Dawn Marie four ever. III. Title:
Robert and Dawn Marie forever.
PZ7.C6628Ro 1986　　[Fic]　　85-45269
ISBN 0-06-021396-5
ISBN 0-06-021397-3 (lib. bdg.)

For Mandy the shining Princess,
and my own boys

The places in this novel are a combination of reality and invention. The characters are purely fictional, and any resemblance to real people is coincidental.

1

"Robert, you're gettin' on my nerves again! Starin' like that. I can't stand how he's lookin' at me! It has got to stop!"

Give me a break. It wouldn't matter if I was staring or I wasn't. What they really want is for me just not to be there.

"Now, honey, take it easy," Joe says. "Tell him you'll send him back to the foster home if he don't act right. You got plenty to do taking care of the baby." My mother's boyfriend pops another can of beer, about his tenth. "Apartment's getting too crowded anyway. Kid his age, he could make out by hisself."

My mother starts fussing in the mirror with her "Sheena—The Jungle Girl" hair; it's long, like she's still sixteen. I figure she's about thirty, 'cause I'm fourteen. My little brother starts crying in the bedroom.

"Oh, they're not really brothers," she tells people in the Laundromat. "Robert's just a half brother. His father run away soon's he knew about Robert. Worst thing I ever did, letting that man get within six blocks a me. That was my biggest mistake."

So what else is new? Getting born was *my* biggest mistake.

She usually lets the baby cry a lot longer, but she runs into the bedroom this time. I'm trying not to look at Joe. It's hairy being alone in the room with him. He was in Vietnam, and he acts like he's still there, all wound up tight, waiting for somebody to start something. Wouldn't make any difference if there was a Vietnam or there wasn't. Some guys are always looking for a war. With Joe putting away all that beer, I figure this is a good time to head for the project playground, fifteen stories down.

The halls aren't any dirtier than usual—same empty potato-chip bags and squashed soda cans. The same teenagers making out in the elevator; they don't even look when I get on. The same dumb stuff scrawled all over the hallways. This place is just too big for anybody to worry about keeping it pretty.

In the playground people are sitting with their kids in strollers. The same guys are still dribbling the basketball, jumping up on those long, soda-straw legs, Converse All-Stars coming down hard, *Whop!* They do basketball the way some people do religion.

2

You have to be terrific to even think of asking for a game, and I'm pretty pathetic at sports. So needless to say, I don't ask.

I see Joe's heap at the curb—1974 Chevy with one brown fender, the rest green, a pink plastic rose that used to light up on the antenna. Glad I'm never going to be riding with that mean dude again, gunning through red lights, getting taxi guys cursing at him so he can start swinging. He took off the muffler, and with the tailpipe dragging sparks off the pavement, it's like being in the Vietnam War.

I'm over on Flatbush Avenue now, walking faster and faster, practically running. This is *it*! I'm leaving! All my life they've been shootin' me down like the alien in *Space Invaders*. Social workers, judges, my mother and her boyfriends. You're damn right I can make it by myself, Joe, 'cause I'm my own man now. I'm never going back!

Next to me on the avenue, bashed-in Pontiacs, Plymouths, and huge, old tail-fin Caddies are nosing along fender to fender. The Spanish guys are taking their wives and six kids and the gramma for a Sunday ride. Everybody's holding a kid on their laps, and the gramma's kissing the baby. Nobody's screaming, "Get away! This kid is making me nervous!"

My sneakers just keep on traveling along, going somewhere. I turn onto Fourth, which is one *cold* avenue. It goes on forever, closed-up stores and theaters, buildings crumbling down into the vacant lots. Sky's T.V. white, dead. Bay Ridge over that way, Bensonhurst, Flatbush, Fort Greene, Coney Island. Boy, you name it, I've been in a foster home there. Millions of people in Brooklyn, and they're never going to get out. Maybe a little trip once a year, over the river to Radio City, the Big Time. It's a cemetery, only they're still alive.

My feet just keep pumping. Must be more than an hour since I left. Swinging onto 3rd Street— people sitting on their stoops or leaning back in folding beach chairs on the sidewalk, laughing, imagining they're having a good time. They're going by like I was running in a movie.

Finally I see it up ahead—high, green, dark, a secret country that's in Brooklyn but not in Brooklyn—the park. Big metal lions are walking tough on top of the gates. The road is like a long rug somebody's pulling on. It's running under me; trees are whispering, "This way. This way." I'm never coming out again where the dirty buildings are and the people that look at me like "Oh, Robert. Is *he* still here?" I'll hole up in a cave, make it by myself.

A couple of hours later I know *I'm* never getting out. I'm still here in Brooklyn. The park's got roads everywhere, with jerks speeding around the curves, going through red lights. Too many paths with leftover picnic junk spread all around. Even way in the middle, where it looks bushy and wild, it isn't. Here comes a dumb jogger in his little pants, bouncing along on his toes. And about finding a cave, forget it! Everything's used. Any little hollowed-out place, not even big enough to hide in, is filled with beer cans.

It's getting late. I walk and walk, wherever the path goes. Still feels like winter, even if it's March, and the warm is all worn out of this jacket. I try not to listen to the darkness that's breathing, waiting. Then I hunch up on a bench, my head on my knees, creeping into sleep like I was a dog going in a little house in the backyard.

Sometime in the night I hear wolves running together, scuffling the leaves, biting at each other and snarling. I'm up in the nearest tree, fast! Wrapping myself around the thick main branches, I sleep some more till it's morning and I hear this lady screaming.

"I got nauseous, the smell was so bad! They had to use two of those leaf bags to take the thing away. I mean, this snake was ten feet long! A boa constrictor, yes it was! The park police said so. In this park you could find anything, dead snakes, dead people! It shouldn't be allowed!"

"Must have been somebody's pet."

"Pet?! Such a disgusting thing! Who'd want that for a pet?"

"Somebody must have gotten tired of it and dumped it in the park. Listen, it's one of God's creatures. It can't help it if it's ugly. Some of us aren't so beautiful either." She laughs. The other one doesn't.

They're right under my tree. Pushing away a few dead leaves, I can see the old lady who screams everything. Her hat's wrapped around her head like a towel, holding her orange hair on tight. The collar of her coat *has* to be a dead cat. Looking straight down, I can't see her face, but I know the type. This one's face is gonna be scary white, with red lipstick and eyes all squinty from watching for criminals.

The other one is funny-looking. She has a shape like a bunch of mashed potatoes, especially in this red, stretch-pants outfit she's wearing. Some kind of a furry pancake hat with a Christmas tree pin has crash-landed on her head. And she's standing there in pink running shoes a couple of sizes too big. Oh, man, the thrift shop must love this lady.

Then I notice her Gramma's front porch. You could see a little kid climbing up her and putting his head right down. I got to admit it. She's sort of a nice kind of funny-looking.

"Well, the dogs are waiting for their breakfast. Take care!" She pats Towel Head's arm and moves into the park, carrying a lumpy, Zippy Supermarket shopping bag.

Somebody, when I was little, sounded like that— the day-care teacher in the project. My mother used to pull me along behind her, open the door, aim me at the teacher, and split. I'd be too scared to do anything but just stand there, crying and running at the nose. Then I'd hear, "How you this mornin', Robert darlin'?" I'd push my head into her and she'd hold me against her, not minding the runny nose on her skirt.

6

I stayed about a year, and she kept me from going crazy. You wouldn't think little kids could go crazy, but they can. They look at grown-ups screaming and fighting, and it's like a horror movie to them. After a while the kid goes somewhere inside and doesn't come out anymore. But this lady—I remember her name was Lillian—she'd give us our little cartons of milk and baked macaroni at lunch, and when it was getting dark and the other kids got picked up and my mother still hadn't come, she'd hold me on her lap by the window. We'd watch together. "See, Robert, honey, here comes your mother now! I told you she'd be comin'."

So, who knows? Maybe that's why I drop down out of the tree and follow this Looney Toons lady. My sneakers are real quiet, and I hide behind trees. She has this dopey smile on her face. I bet she just smiles at anybody whether she knows 'em or not. She'd smile at a mugger and ask him how was his day. What a scene! Mugger jumps out at her; she starts babblin' away, and the mugger backs off, mumblin', "Crazy ol' bag!"

Crossing the big space in the middle of the park—there's grass but no trees—I hang pretty far back. She heads for some scraggly bushes and trees where the grass ends. Something's moving there.

Dogs! About ten, dirty white, brown, wolf color; they're going back and forth, heads down, nervous, waiting for something. She takes the Zippy Supermarket bag and empties it on the ground.

"Here I am, children. Now, don't fight. There's

enough for everybody. Poor things, you're about starved." They must have been the wolves I heard in the night.

By now I've caught up and have to go ahead; I'm not interested, see. Where the path turns out of sight, I duck into the bushes and circle back. The dogs are biting and growling at the stuff she put out; you'd think they're killing it. Mostly there's dry, brown kennel-bits, but here and there are halves of Big Macs and fries, messy with ketchup. This lady must have been diving in all the trash cans at McDonald's!

The fried smell is taking me back to hundreds of times waiting for the guy to say, "What'll it be?" You know, your teeth are already chomping through that round, soft bread bun, the green, snappy pickles, the ketchup smacked out of the bottle, and then, oozing juice, the sizzled, flattened-down burger. I was really tasting that burger! In fact, I forgot I was hiding.

"What's your name, boy? Are you in the park by yourself? Are you lost? No, I guess you're too big for that. Well, you look about as hungry as one of these dogs. Wait till I give 'em the last of their food, and we'll go home and get you something to eat—unless your folks'll be looking for you?"

I shake my head hard. They're not gonna be looking for me. And they're not gonna sic the cops on me either, 'cause then they might have to take me back.

"What'd you say your name was?"

I think about saying "Frank" or "John" or "Smoky Joe," but I say, "Robert."

"Robert, what a nice Scottish name! I'm Margaret Mary. Scottish, French, English on my mother's side, Irish on my husband Walter Murphy's side. Robert, would you pick up those bits of paper and trash, now the dogs are through? Oh, there's the black one. Pretend you don't see him. He's got too much pride to come and eat with the rest. We'll just put some food down over near him, and he'll come for it when we're gone. Prince, that's what I call him. Maybe he once was a Prince, but now he's got to be an outlaw."

That dog doesn't look like any Prince to me. His black hair is spiky and dirty. His head is down and he doesn't look proud; he just looks vicious, glaring at us with his flat, yellow eyes. They don't beg though, the way the other dogs' eyes did: "Please, please, I'm a nice doggy! Like me!" He's a mean dude, an outlaw like she said.

"Well." She's talking again. "We're going to get you fed. How long have you been in the park? Oh, now, it doesn't matter atall how long. What you need, Robert, is some *good* breakfast. Come on now."

I start after her, across the grassy space, and she keeps turning around and talking to me.

"I come every other day or so to feed the dogs. Would you believe people just throw their dogs away, drive into the park and push 'em out of the car?"

I'd believe it.

"It didn't use to be like that. When I was a girl,

9

I used to come in the park, and it looked so peaceful and sort of way back in time. Why, I used to think I was going to see Dutchmen with those big lace collars, talking to some serious Indians with bare chests. That's what it showed in my fourth-grade reader, you know. But I never did," and she smiled like she was looking at herself back there, a little girl.

By now we're at the benches on the edge of the park, facing the avenue. She waves to a row of sitters.

"Gloria! I haven't seen you for a week! How've you been? Robert, this is Gloria. Gloria, this is Robert. Gloria lives in those apartments over there, and she is a good friend and a real nice person. I'm taking Robert home for some breakfast. Eggs and oatmeal. Do you like oatmeal, Robert?"

Gloria's the one on the end with the poodle. It's been washed so much, you can see the rubbed, pink skin through the white. Gloria's eyes x-ray me all over, stopping at every hole in my jacket and sneakers. This Margaret Mary thinks everybody is her friend, but if you ask me, she doesn't know who's her friend and who's her enemy.

We go on down the avenue, and I don't have to look back to know Gloria's telling the other "girls" on the bench, "I just expect a person to be clean and neat. It's not too much to ask. Poor Margaret Mary's kind of a mess herself, so I guess she doesn't know the difference. She's got herself another stray dog."

Margaret Mary's shuffling down the avenue, breathing like it hurts someplace. But she keeps bending over, picking up papers and trash to put in the litter baskets on the corners. She sees me watching. "I know it seems crazy, but it makes Brooklyn look a little better." She smiles, so I nod my head.

I'm saying to myself, "Just isn't that much to smile about all the time. I better start thinking about getting away from this ol' wacko-spacko dame. Soon as I get something to eat, I'll start working on some plans."

We turn off the avenue, away from the brown four-story buildings stuck together going on in a line as far as you can see. You've got them all over Brooklyn, but these by the park are fancier. A lot of them are white, smooth, white steps going up to the glass doors with shiny gold door handles. Long, polished glass windows with white curtains stare at the park. Nobody's looking out, and you don't see the big-shot types who live there either; probably they're too important to come out. And they don't make noise.

Going down 16th Street there's plenty of people and noise. Little kids, bunches of them, playing on the sidewalk, hanging on to the baby buggies their mothers are pushing. "Stop crying or I'll smack you. Here, you want a Popsicle?" Old Pontiacs are getting fixed at the curb, and teenagers sit on the hoods, their eyes cruising up and down the block.

The houses get smaller and more separate, the

11

way kids draw houses. It's like a family was in there, and they decided, "Hey, this house would look good pink!" And their pop painted it, and then he put a little green plastic awning over the front door. And then he went to Sears and got that green rug grass to cover his yard. So it was dinky, six feet by eight feet maybe, but he'd have a nice, neat, green yard all winter.

We go past blue houses and green ones, and sometimes there's a straight, flat-roof one with tar paper on the sides and bricks drawn on with a ruler. And on every block, there's one house like a rotten tooth, its insides showing. Kids have broken all the windows and they'll keep breaking it up, taking away bricks and smashing stuff till it isn't a house anymore.

Margaret Mary's still going, waving to everybody, stopping to ask this little, bent-over guy sweeping his sidewalk, "How's your blood pressure, Carl?" And telling a fat lady, "Mrs. Rizzo, you must have lost fifteen pounds! You look *beautiful!*" It's sort of embarrassing, but I don't have anything better to do at the moment, do I?

Now we're at this low wall, and you can see down a long yard that's really weird. There's little raggedy trees and bushes with fake birds tied in them. Brown-painted speckled deer statues, standing and lying down, nesting in the old, dead leaves and grass. Little plaster rabbits and squirrels chase each other between toy wooden windmills. There's a doll buggy with an old rubber doll in it. One of those snooty, long-legged, pink birds is looking down at some yellow and green plastic flowers planted in a rubber tire. The tire is snipped so points hang down all around, and it's painted silver. This has got to be Margaret Mary's house.

Sure enough, she cranks open a fussy old gate and I follow her down the walk. By the house there's a church statue, the Virgin Mary I guess, in a plaster seashell that curves over her. She's looking out with her hand raised, over Snow White and the Seven Dwarfs, Thumper, Bambi, and lots of other little Disney animals.

Margaret Mary waves me to come on. She stops to straighten a rusty, spotted enamel coffeepot she's got planted with some old weeds, then climbs up on this little porch strung with yellow and red plastic party lanterns. Weirder and weirder! I'd split if I wasn't so hungry.

She pulls off her hat, showing a lot of gray hair pinned up in funny bunches. You know she didn't look in the mirror when she was doing it. Then she opens the door and a brownish, middle-sized dog and a striped cat come rushing out. The dog is old and fat, so she doesn't rush very fast. She starts licking Margaret Mary's knee, which is as high as she can reach. The cat grins and leans its head on her boot.

"Walter!" Margaret Mary shouts. "I've brought us a boy!"

2

Here it comes. This old crock she's married to, he's going to come out of wherever he is, shake his head, and say, "Looks like a mean one." I'm just waiting to see which door it'll be. There are more doors in here than any house could ever use, and more old sofas and different kinds of chairs than anybody could ever sit in. There's lots of other stuff, limpy tables with china Scottie dogs, and ashtrays that are lying-down girls in bathing suits with one leg up. Margaret Mary must never throw *anything* away.

Walter comes out of the kitchen holding a newspaper. This guy is *big*! Fuzzy gray hair rings around his mostly bald head, which he has to bend to get through the door. He's got a stomach like Santa Claus, but muscles in his arms like he works out with the weights.

14

"Yes, oh, yes!" he says, and he's smiling the same dopey way that she smiles.

"Walter, this is Robert. Robert, this is Walter." She heads for the kitchen, babbling over her shoulder. "Robert was in the park and he helped me feed the dogs. Then he was nice enough to visit us for breakfast, be our guest, so to speak. Maybe he'd even stay a bit longer, if he likes it here." What's she talking about? How does she know I won't hit her on the head and rob the house? Not that there's anything here anybody would want to rob.

"Sit down, won't you, Robert?" He pulls up a big cushioned chair for me. "I see in the papers here, the Sixers dusted the Knicks, again. Wasn't that a shame!" Catching that I'm not exactly interested in sports, he starts on something else in the *Daily News*. "This feller here, he won the lottery, and he didn't even know it! Sent his pants to the cleaners with the ticket right in the pocket. Mother-in-law calls him up, 'Didn't you pick number so-and-so, that was your oldest child's birthday and your anniversary?' 'Yeah,' he says. And she's screaming, 'That's it! You won, you boob!' Well, he gets to the cleaners like he was shot out of a cannon, and it was there, right in that pocket! Went through the cleaning machine and everything."

I have to smile a little, thinking of this guy screeching around the corners to the cleaners. By now there's a crispy brown—well, black—smell curling out of the kitchen. She's singing and burn-

15

ing the bacon. My stomach is on its knees, begging. There's a cozy racket of dishes being smacked down, the fridge door opening and shutting. "Just come along, Robert! Breakfast's ready!" she yells.

Walter gets up and starts nudging me into the kitchen, smiling down from what I guess is six foot six. More mess and junk, but it's not dirty. I'm used to mess and dirt. My mother never can get herself to cleaning up day before yesterday's supper, let alone last night's. This kitchen's just full of *stuff*. There are three or four toasters, antique models; it turns out none of them work. The walls are hanging with doll-size frying pans that say things like "Atlantic City" and "New Jersey's Ocean Playground," a John F. Kennedy and a Robert Kennedy plate, also curly metal hearts you put hot pots on. "Kiss Me I'm Irish," a big green button, is pinned on the curtain. There's a sewed picture of a little house with sewed words: "If my husband should chance to roam, give him a beer and send him home." Oh, and glass jars and coffee cans of dry dirt with big pits stuck into them. Only one was crazy enough to send up a poke of green. Margaret Mary probably forgot to water them.

I don't hang around long looking at the kitchen. Two bull's-eye eggs, four slices of bacon, and a bowl of oatmeal are looking at *me*—"What are you waiting for? We're ready!" I could cry, it tastes so good, except I never cry.

Margaret Mary and Walter sit at the table watching proudly: "Just look at that boy eat!" I try not

16

to snatch and swallow too much. Then she asks me would I like a glass of milk, a cup of coffee, or both.

"Won't your folks be worried about you, Robert?" I look at the plate hard, knowing I have to say something to Walter.

"My mother's dead. I never had a father." I'm lying myself silly. But they don't know what day it is. If they get wise, I'll just take off somewhere.

"Ohhh, say, that's real sad." This guy's eyes actually get tears in them.

"Where've you been staying?"

He wouldn't want to know all the places: Aunt Alice's dark, brown living room, next to the funeral parlor, me sitting by the window because "Auntie Alice doesn't like noisy boys jumpin' around." I'd be watching the long, slick black cars, the men in black suits putting the box in the car with no windows. . . . Then there's the court judge leaning over, his glasses throwing sharp splinters in my eyes. "We have a juvenile here, in need of supervision. Remand him to Children's Center." And the man— he has a gun in a leather strap on his white shirt— hands me to a lady who's waiting. He talks to her with the side of his mouth, but I hear, "Mother don't want him. Another 'throwaway.' " And I start crying and kicking and biting, partly 'cause I'm scared of the gun, partly 'cause of what he said.

"He never acts like that!" says my mother. "Stop it now, Robert! I'll come get you pretty soon, *only* if you're good." It was five years and six foster homes till she did.

17

By then I almost wished she hadn't. She never did get any older than a teenager. Some women are just kids themselves, with a doll. When the doll makes them nervous, they just throw it on the ground. That's why I wasn't jealous of the baby. I was sorry for what was going to happen to him, and I told him funny stories and patted his head when she wasn't around.

"He doesn't want to answer all these questions now, do you, Robert? Why don't you go read your paper in the parlor while I clean up, Walter? Robert can help me."

"I can take out your garbage. Or go to the store. Whatever you need," I tell her.

"Just keep me company for a bit," she says, "while I clean up this kitchen. Then I'll give you some jobs to do." She rinses the dishes and fusses around, picking things up, putting them down in a different place. It doesn't look any neater when she's done.

"Do you know what Walter is? Could you guess?" Before I can answer, she says, "He's a champion, a real champion."

"Heavy-weight boxer?"

"No, indeed! He's the gold-medal national roller-skating champion of the whole United States—1939 and '40. He might teach you some roller-skating if you asked him. But he's shy about telling people he's a champion."

Roller-skating doesn't seem that much to me— little kids bent over waving their arms, going too fast down the sidewalk.

"Oh," she says. "You don't know how pretty it can be. It's artistic. They do these jumps and turns with their arms like this." She throws out her arms and knocks the Atlantic City frying pan off the wall. "I must look like Dumbo, the baby elephant." She kind of blushes. "But Walter is—magnificent! You'll see.

"Here." She goes in a drawer and pulls out a pocketbook that looks like she's had it since 1939. "Here's five dollars. If you would go to the big Zippy Supermarket over on Eighth Avenue and 5th Street and get me some more of this Suds-Bright—the giant size, it's much more economical—I would appreciate it. And close the gate so the dog can't get out. Heather-Belle doesn't see too well, and she'd get run over sure."

When I'm going down the path, I bet she's already thinking it's a mistake she gave me the five dollars; maybe I won't come back. The gate has to be hitched up to meet the catch, which is a twisted wire on a nail. I do it carefully for Heather-Belle. Along the top of the wall, where most people would put broken glass or metal spikes, she's got a parade of dinky little wind-up toys. Kids don't even bother to steal them, they're so rusty and busted up.

The neighborhood kids I see are like anywhere in Brooklyn. They're little fat girls, and their mothers dress them up cute and shove them outside to sit on the stoop. "Don't go nowhere, or I'll break your legs." And little guys, skinny from running all the time, and finding stuff in the lots, and dragging it somewhere else for an army fort. When they grow up, the little girls don't listen to their mothers anymore. They start hanging out down at the corner with the guys who used to play army. Only now the guys are fixing up old Plymouths and Chevys with fins, and leaning their jeans against the hoods. And the girls are leaning their jeans next to the guys.

I don't have to worry about making it with these kids. I'm only in the neighborhood awhile, then I'm gone. They don't mess with me, and I don't mess with them. Maybe because I'm a loner, they think I'm a crazy who'll suddenly just go wild, start swinging, get 'em back for all the times they looked around me like nobody was walking by. But don't worry, guys, it's not my style.

Paul Newman's my man—Cool Hand Luke. They can't get to him because he's COOL. Doesn't say much. Just gives the mean dudes this little grin, blue eyes laughing at the corners. I guess I've seen about every picture of his at least ten times on the late night movie. He's really tough, like when they threw him in the shed for a couple of days and nights without water or anything. It was so hot, and he never said a word. When he talks, he does it so nice. These guys around here in Brooklyn are always talking big, "Yo' mother" and "I'm gonna bust ya inna mouth." That's all they ever say.

Funny coincidence—my eyes are blue. If I could have an older brother, I'd pick him. We could hang out, have some good times together. Yeah . . . well, Suds-Bright.

On the corner there's this huge, yellow-brick chunk of a building with crosses on top. St. Saviour's it says over the door. Right next to it another yellow-brick building with green cutout tulips, every one traced the same, pasted on long rows of windows. It's got to be a school. The crossing guard comes down the street dressed like a cop, except she's got a lot of makeup on, and her hair sprayed into a Jackie Kennedy, with this dumb white-and-navy hat on top of it.

Must be noon. The sisters stand at the door letting the Catholic school kids out. They start running and fooling, and the mothers who've been waiting scream, "Michael! Get back here! Stop punching your sister or you're gonna get it!"

Then around the corner there's a burst of high school girls laughing and shaking their long hair around their faces. "No!! Now, Lisa! You know I can't *stand* him! He's a jerk!" More screams and laughing. "Get rid of that cigarette—Sister might be looking out of the window!" The kid with the cigarette holds it in two fingers like it was alive and getting ready to bite. As soon as they're across the street, she sticks it between her lips, which are so red they come at you way before the rest of her face.

The girls are all wearing these little plaid skirts pulled up to show their knees. And that's a mistake,

21

because most of the knees are red, and too fat or too bony. Except one pair—they're on these legs that are long and straight, not too straight, I mean they curve down to these two really nice feet in loafers. (I'm traveling along among them, but like I said, I'm not the kind people see.) Now I'm taking a sideways glance at her face: straight dark kind of eyebrows, her eyes looking down—I guess because she feels me looking at her—no lipstick, just her own pink lips, two tiny pearl earrings. There's a pearliness all around her that makes *me* have to look at the ground.

"Dawn M'ree! Dawn M'ree! Wait!" A girl with a long black pigtail and a soft brown face comes charging up. Indian, the kind whose father has a little clothing store and her mother wears a long wrapped dress with a sweater over it. She grabs Dawn Marie's arm. "What did Sister say about the French homework? Is it due Thursday? Come have lunch at my house and we'll work on it."

They're swirled away into the mob. I just catch the long black pigtail and *her* hair—dark, kind of fluffy and ripply, way down her back. And she's gone.

Dawn Marie. Dawn Marie. Dawn—it sounds like she looks. Talking to myself, I walk right past the supermarket and have to go back. The manager—I know that's who he is because he's always watching—gives me that "Lousy, shoplifting kids. I know you and I got my eye on you" look.

"Sucker, you don't know me at all," I breathe.

22

And I see me and my buddy, Paul Newman, happy as can be, just bending up all his shopping carts. You know, like Paul did in *Cool Hand Luke*, with the parking meters. Bent 'em over like daisies!

Where's this soap she wants, Suds-Bright, giant size? It's always on T.V. I start thinking of Margaret Mary going on T.V. for Suds-Bright: "Here she is, ladies and gentlemen, Mrs. Margaret Mary Murphy, who's going to show us how she uses Suds-Bright!" And Margaret Mary's got her dippy hat on, and she's blinking out of the screen, and you don't know which is her and which is the pile of old laundry. I'm grinning and then my face goes hot. It wasn't funny when she was saying, "What you need, Robert, is some *good* breakfast."... "This young man was nice enough to visit us."... "Would you like a glass of milk, a cup of coffee, or both?"

To make it up to her, I burn the pavement getting back. Walter's sitting in a La-Z-Boy lounger with the plastic peeling off, and Margaret Mary's rocking in a bumpy rocker. They look up, smiling like I'm something special to see. She says, "Thank you, Robert. It was so kind of you." Walter's getting up from his La-Z-Boy. "Time to show those pots down at the restaurant who's boss. See you at suppertime, Robert."

"Nice guy," I think. People that nice must have something wrong with them. Something must be missing that they don't see all the mean dudes cruising out there. Maybe the men in the white coats are going to drive up and take them to the funny farm.

But meanwhile I've got to admit it—they're sort of cute, Margaret Mary and Walter.

The rest of the day I pick up in the yard, scratching with the rake and sweeping clouds of dust and twigs off the walk onto the old, dead grass. Mostly, I straighten up and clean the fake rabbits and squirrels, a mama duck with a string of little ducks behind her, and the windmills with cutout wooden people. Miss Muffet with the spider—I remember being scared of the picture with that spider in the day-care center. Only it would have been a cockroach, or a rat, that scared Miss Muffet if she lived where I used to. Hey, now I don't live anywhere. I just hang around awhile till they're through with me.

Heather-Belle follows me around, smiling with her lips pulled back. She's pretty fat and old. After a while she flops on her side on the torn quilt Margaret Mary puts out on the step for her. I'm glad when it's five o'clock and the gate's complaining about letting Walter in.

Sitting at the supper table, in my mind I take pictures, pictures I'll need when I'm out in the dark somewhere. Margaret Mary feeds the cat and dog first. "I hope you don't mind, Robert. The poor creatures don't know why they have to wait. It's hard with the sights and smells right in front of them."

Big Boy, the cat, is walking around on the counter, bowing down and pumping with his paws, while she scrapes out the Pretty Kitty, fish flavor, into his dish.

24

Heather-Belle sits grinning up at Margaret Mary, who is squeezing something out of a dropper on her dog food. "It's her heart medicine. She's eleven years old, you know."

"Wait till you taste Margaret Mary's cookin'." Walter nudges me. "She could cook up a rubber boot and it'd be tasty."

Margaret Mary laughs. "You're not telling that boy we're having a rubber boot for supper, are you? Don't worry, Robert." And she comes puffing to the table with a speckled enamel stewpot that's steaming out good news. She gives me a huge dipperful and another on top of it. Walter and Margaret Mary eat and talk, smiling at me.

"Hon', I saw Mrs. Polini and Marsha today. They got back from Disneyland, and Mrs. Polini says Mickey Mouse shook Marsha's hand and she was chattering away to him. They had to hold on to her or she'd have followed him all over Disneyland. Mrs. Polini was just crying, she was so happy." (Why would this lady cry about her little kid talking to Mickey Mouse?)

Walter nods, "Yes, oh, yes."

I figure I ought to say something about now. "You sure make good stew," I mumble.

"Well, that's just what we've been needing around here, a hungry boy. Not that Walter isn't a good eater." She leans over and pats his stomach.

Stuffed with stew and a raspberry bakery bun and a cheese one, too, I'm blinking in the warm kitchen light. I'd like to be doing what Big Boy is,

25

sleeping on a lumpy chair cushion, paws tucked under his chest. He looks like a little boat on some waves. But I ought to be making some plans.

My head is dropping when I hear Margaret Mary say, "Walter, Robert must be awfully tired. Why don't you show him where his bed is?"

My bed? You'd think they knew I was coming. I tell her, "I can do the dishes."

She waves me up the stairs behind Walter. I don't know what I'm getting into, but for tonight, I might as well.

"In here, Robert. This is the guest room."

I'm looking just inside the door at a big old refrigerator with a pink lampshade tossed on top.

"I hope you don't mind. Seems just too good to throw out. And like Margaret Mary says, someday it just might take to working again."

"Oh no, I don't mind."

"That's a studio bed," Walter says, "and there's plenty more covers right here. See you in the morning."

This place is a furniture store, only they'd never get any customers. It's full of stuff Margaret Mary's saving. Probably because she's sorry for it. Plenty of out-of-work chairs, including a fat old one with a big hat covering the seat. I guess that's to keep you from sitting on it, because the springs have been sat right out the bottom. This hat is a big, dippy straw job with a moldy bird sitting on it. It must be from the Civil War. Oh, and there's crying and happy clown pictures all over the walls, and a browned-out photograph of some dude in a Charlie Chaplin hat. He's next to a lady pulled in tight in the middle so everything gets squeezed up to the top.

Going sideways past a bureau with a missing mirror, I flip out the light and fall into bed. Rabbits, squirrels, and wooden windmill people gather around smiling at me.

"Doesn't say much, does he?"

"Oh, but he's such a nice boy, and handsome, too."

Margaret Mary's and Walter's voices are floating up out of the floor. (Next day I see there's a hot-air register going down through the kitchen to the furnace.)

"Now, don't get upset, Margaret Mary, but we're probably going to have to tell the police or somebody he's here. It's against the law to just keep a child."

I'm sitting up like an electric buzzer went off.

"Walter! Can't you see he's run away from something? Cruelty, most likely. Do I tell the A.S.P.C.A. when I find a dog lost in the streets or starving in the park? No! Because the A.S.P.C.A.'ll just have to kill 'em! They try, but there's so many lost. Well, I'm not turning this boy over to be killed! You heard what he said, his mother's dead and he never had a father. Are we going to send him to the institution, to an orphanage?!"

"No, oh, no! But we've got to give him back to wherever he belongs, you know that, Margaret Mary.

In a day or so I'll just go down to the police station. There's this fellow, Al. He's a V.F.W. buddy of mine, and he's the desk sergeant. I'll find out from him what the law says we're supposed to do. Wait a minute. Guess it'll have to be next Friday, because I told 'em I could take two shifts next coupla' days at the restaurant. Boss is out sick. Meanwhile, I don't see why the boy just couldn't have a little vacation here with us, like they send kids to camp to get the fresh air."

"Oh, next Friday would be the best." Margaret Mary starts running on. "Now, he'll need some nice clothes; that jacket has seen better days. And I'll have to find out some of his favorite foods. Boys need nutrition, because they're growing all the time, you know. Wouldn't want him to get growing pains from not enough nutrition or anything like that."

She's going on and on. I just slide back down and pull a thick quilt of sleep over my head. I've got nine days till next Friday, and that's a lo-o-o-ong time.

3

"Robert! Oh, Robert! There's somebody here to see you! Come on down!" Sun is fingering my eyelids. . . . I finally figure out who's screaming at me. Sleeping in your clothes, it's no problem getting dressed, and I'm stumbling down the stairs in no time.

Funny, the kitchen doesn't look messy to me anymore. It looks just the way a kitchen should. The sunshine's coming in, turning the few green leaves in the coffee can greeny gold. It's shining up the toasters and stroking Big Boy's orange stripes on the windowsill, where he's closing his eyes, feeling good.

Margaret Mary is standing there, holding somebody's arm who's smiling a lot. Is it an old lady or an old kid? This person's got kind of Chinese eyes and a too-small head on a body that's too heavy toward the bottom, and she's hugging a red toy telephone. I think, if she's a kid, why has she got wrinkles? I'm trying not to stare, but this is giving me queer, mixed-up feelings. Margaret Mary just goes right on.

"Robert, this is Marsha. Remember I said she went to Disneyland with her folks? Marsha, do you want to say something to Robert on your telephone? Go ahead, hon'."

Marsha's smiling and holding out the telephone to me, so I take it and put it to my ear. She's waiting for me to say something. "Uh, I hear you've been to Disneyland, and you saw Mickey Mouse?"

Her face practically splits in half, she's smiling so much now. She grabs the phone back and starts talking. "Mickey Mouse! You said Marsha's a good girl. You said, 'I like to see you some more. Come see me, Marsha.' I love you, Mickey Mouse!"

She runs out of the kitchen all excited, and Margaret Mary calls after her, "Go straight home, dear! She lives right next door. She knows the way, and she's very good at minding."

Margaret Mary sits down across from me while I'm spooning in the oatmeal, something I never liked too much, but she's looking at me so pleased, what can I do?

"Marsha . . ." she says, "Marsha is the Polinis' daughter. She's thirty-seven, the only child they ever had. And I know there're some people who say they'd be better off if they'd never had any children, Marsha being the way she is. Or they say to put her in an institution. But you know, she has the sweetest nature, just loves everybody. And every little thing she learns to do, her mother just cries, she's so proud. Sad, too, I guess. But your child is your child; nothing can ever change that. Nothing can ever make you put that child away from you."

Oh, sure, tell me about it. I don't ask, but there's such a pain in her eyes, I think I know why there's no photographs around of little kids in a new suit with a bow tie or a white fluffy dress. She and Walter must have never had any kids. I look away, then quickly take my bowl to the sink.

Margaret Mary gets up on her feet, sighing on account of her sore legs. She grins at me. "Won't get any parsnips buttered sitting here." She starts puttering at the sink. "You know, Robert, you're welcome to stay awhile if you need to."

"I can get a job," I say. "There's lots of newspapers people throw out, and I could collect them with one of those supermarket carts and take them to a depot and sell them." That's the most I've spoken since coming here, and it spills out fast. If I bring them some money, maybe I can hold off Margaret Mary and Walter from saying, "We just don't want you here anymore."

"Well, that's a good idea, son. Walter'd know how you do it, where the depot is and all. Would you mind taking Heather-Belle for a walk? She'd just sit her life away, clogging up her arteries. You can get to know the neighborhood, too."

Heather-Belle is swaying slowly down the street,

about one half mile per hour. "Son." She must not have been thinking what she was saying! It's just another word people use for "kid." Meanwhile, I'm feeling like Big Boy on the windowsill.

It's about ten o'clock. Up near the park, it's the time all the old men and old ladies come out to walk their old-man and old-lady dogs. Hats, they're all wearing hats, even when it's almost spring. Turned-over pots, velvet maybe, with gold circle pins for the ladies, and checked stingy brims for a couple of sporty guys. Mostly it's regular-gray hats, too big for old guys who have shrunk. They're carrying and walking little, snappy Mexican dogs with popping eyes, and miniature poodles.

Back in my neighborhood (I mean Margaret Mary's), I see there's more of the Heather-type dog—droopy, featherduster tail, a build like a sofa, and old, milky-brown eyes, looking far away instead of for other dogs.

I figure Heather-Belle's about ready for her quilt when I hear, "Robert, you come here!" It's Marsha, sitting on her front steps, a smile button with wrinkles. What you say to a person like Marsha kind of worries me, but she pats the step beside her. "You sit," and I sit. Heather-Belle sighs herself down and starts licking Marsha's knee.

For a while we just watch the street going by. She's hanging on to her red telephone and waving "Hi!" to everybody. Some people wave back. "Hi, Marsha!" Others stiffen up and pretend they don't hear. It's peaceful, sitting there. Then Marsha pushes her telephone into my lap.

"You talk. You talk."

What should I say? I worry people might think, "Maybe he's like Marsha?" But they already look at me funny, so who cares?

"Hello, Marsha?" She claps her hands. "Marsha, this is Robert. How ya doin'?"

She grabs the phone back. "I'm calling up Mickey Mouse. Mickey Mouse? He's not there! Where are you, Mickey Mouse?" I think she's going to cry.

"Hey now, Marsha, he'll be right back. He just went to visit his friend, Donald Duck. He'll be right back." Why am I saying all this stuff? I'm famous for not saying anything: "That kid gives me the creeps, staring at me. He never talks like a regular kid. You got to do something about him or you get yourself another dude to pay the rent."

Marsha is leaning over looking up in my face. "Robert, you good boy." She takes my hand and holds it.

"Marsha! It's lunchtime! Oh, I hope she didn't bother you." Mrs. Polini is the most worried-looking lady I ever saw. She starts apologizing and trying to lift Marsha off the step and haul her in the house, but when Marsha was getting bigger, Mrs. Polini must have been getting smaller. Mrs. Polini hasn't got a chance, especially since Marsha doesn't want to go anywhere.

"Stay with Robert," she says.

"Marsha." I pat her hand. "I'm going to have lunch too. I'll see you soon." Mrs. Polini looks so grateful, it's embarrassing.

Margaret Mary is sitting at the kitchen table in a shiny ocean of aluminum foil. There are little statues and animals and toys in boxes everywhere.

"Easter's coming, you know, Robert. It's only March, but I always like to get my display out early. It's sort of a shrine, you know. Maybe you think rabbits and such don't belong at a shrine?" I wasn't thinking anything. "Well, you see, I feel the little creatures like that should be in it too. They take whatever God gives them and never complain. And suffering hurts the same, if it's a paw caught in a trap or Jesus' poor, nailed hands. At least *I* think so."

I don't know about religious things. I guess I never worry about churches and Jesus and God up there. There's too much real stuff right here, trying to put me down.

The rest of the afternoon, after hot dogs and macaroni, we work fixing up her shrine. She's ripped open this big cardboard box she found that a stove came in, and we cover it inside and out with the aluminum foil. Some places she crinkles it. "That gives a nice effect, don't you think, Robert?" Then we Scotch tape these purple Easter cards—pictures of lilies and bunnies and Easter eggs—all over the inside of the box. Next, on the bottom, she puts down a bunch of the green cellophane grass that goes in Easter baskets. When that's patted down

34

nice, she puts a two-dollar-fifty-size card in the middle—"Greetings to You at Easter Time," with a picture of Jesus' mother holding her little baby. A sheet of purple cellophane comes down over them.

"Hand me that box of toys, please, Robert." Out come a tricycle-riding Easter bunny, a bunny on skis, four old-fashioned bunnies in a Packard convertible, and real-looking rabbits made out of fuzzy cloth. Miniature china horses and dogs, too. Tiny and big, pretty new or saved for a lot of years, they're putting on a little show on this silver, shiny stage.

We carry it carefully out to the yard and put it near the wall, "so people going by can enjoy it." People going by are liable to think somebody's nuts, but Marsha's looking through the fence and she squeals for joy.

"Come on over, Marsha. I've got something nice for you to see," Margaret Mary calls. And the gate groans open for Marsha and a dark puff of hair, straight eyebrows over eyes—this time I can see them—the color of pansies, brown velvet pansies.

"Hi, Dawn Marie. Dawn Marie, I'd like you to meet Robert. Robert, this is Dawn Marie. She lives around the block in back of us on Seventh Avenue. Are you minding Marsha, hon'?"

"Mrs. Polini needed to go to the white sale at A&S, so I told her I'd be glad to take care of Marsha."

I'm gazing at Dawn Marie like a real sap.

"Will you be going to school around here, Robert?" Plain and nice she says it, not looking slantways or touching her hair or doing any of those teenage, girl-boy things. You know, they pretend to be mad— "I tol' you, take your hands offa me!" And then they laugh because they really like it that the guy touched their shoulder.

She's standing there in this ugly Catholic-school uniform—dark-green knee sox; straight, no-shape pleated skirt; the man's kind of white shirt—and she's beautiful. "Stop thinking like this!" I tell myself. "Cut it out! You're a charity case, like Marsha. You're going to go exactly nowhere with this girl."

She's waiting for me to answer. Margaret Mary rushes in.

"Oh, he's just visiting right now, taking a little vacation, so to speak. He'll have to get settled first, make some plans about what he wants to do, you know."

Plans? I haven't come up with any yet, but she makes me sound so important, I turn red. Dawn Marie'll think I'm trying to act like a big-time operator. But she's listening as if it's the truth, that I'm a person who's got plans!

"Yeah, well, I haven't made up my mind. I have to work out a couple of things, things I might want to do, you know."

She nods. "I've got to take Marsha back now, in case her mother comes. She might worry where Marsha is."

"Robert, why don't you go next door too?" says Margaret Mary. "You both can get acquainted."

36

I stumble along behind Dawn Marie and Marsha, trying to be cool.

When we're sitting on the front steps, Marsha brings out her telephone. She and Dawn Marie have a chat.

"What did you see at Disneyland, Marsha?"

"Oh! Oh! I saw Mickey Mouse. . . ." And Marsha's off on her favorite subject. After a minute she pokes the phone at me. "You talk."

"You know you can see Mickey Mouse on the T.V. sometimes on Saturday mornings, Marsha?"

She bumps up and down. "I see him! I see him on T.V.!"

Dawn Marie is smiling toward Marsha. "She really loves Mickey Mouse."

"Mickey's her friend," I say. "Most kids wouldn't want to be."

Dawn Marie nods.

"Remember those old cartoons with Mighty Mouse? These baby birds would always be falling out of their nests, and the bulldog was gonna get them, and Mighty Mouse would save them?"

"Oh sure. I used to love those."

"He'd sock this bulldog, or anything that was bothering this baby bird, right up into the sky. I used to watch Mighty Mouse all the time, and I'd wish I could do that—just take anybody who was mean to a little kid and sock him so hard, he'd wind up flattened out and rolled up like a window shade like they always do in the cartoons." Is this *me*, back-

37

and-forthing conversation like a regular person?

"Do you remember the little-old-shoemaker car-toons?" Dawn Marie says. "He was so poor, but he gave his supper to this dumb little penguin. And what did that penguin always say? I forget."

"*Sneep. Sneep!*"

She laughs. "Yes! That was it!"

Mrs. Polini's standing in front of us, behind a huge tied-up A&S package.

"Oh, you're so nice to mind Marsha for me."

Marsha almost knocks her over, hugging her. Then she lays her head on her mother's chest. "Ma! Ma!"

And Margaret Mary is calling, "Robert, come home! Supper's ready!"

I back away. "I've got to go," and almost land on my head, tripping over a little pebble.

"Oh, be careful," Dawn Marie says.

"Don't worry, I will."

Heather-Belle is waddling down the walk to meet me. For no reason I pick her up (she weighs about a ton) and start waltzing around. Is she surprised! And she's a little scared, so carefully I put her down again. She gives me a hurt look over her shoulder and squeezes under the steps.

Supper is codfish cakes, and mashed potatoes and cabbage mashed together.

"When I was little, I used to squash 'em together. The green looked so nice in the white," Margaret Mary says.

It sounds weird but it tastes good. And for dessert

we each get our own package with two Twinkies. "I know that's a favorite of boys," she says, smiling at me.

"It's a favorite of men, too." Walter pops a whole one in his mouth, swallows, and pats his stomach. It's like he's doing a trick for a little kid, but I grin anyway.

Then the grin gets wiped off my face. Something's *got* to happen to wreck this. Al, down at the police station, he'll tell 'em. I'm a hard-case status offender. You don't have to *do* any crime. Just by being a kid with no real home, that's what you are. Nobody wants you 'cause you're too much trouble. Margaret Mary and Walter must be fooling themselves that I'm worth bothering about. Maybe she's even fooling herself into thinking I could be her kid.

"Robert," Walter is saying, "have you ever roller-skated?"

"Not very much."

"Well, tonight I've got a surprise for you. I'm taking you to the Roller Paradise!"

"That's where Walter teaches on Thursday nights. He does it free for the young people, just so they're serious about wanting to learn. I told you he'd teach you, too. That is, if you'd like it."

"Would you like that, Robert?" Walter asks.

"Sure," I tell him. "Sure." But tonight I sort of wanted to just hang around, remembering how Dawn Marie laughed when I did the penguin sound.

4

—ROLLER PARADISE RINK—
NO GANG JACKETS,
NO WEAPONS
SEARCHES WILL BE MADE

The rink's a dark, square brick block with that sign in front. Behind a giant glass window people, teenagers mostly, are scooting by doing turns, grabbing each other, falling down and laughing, really laughing. You can hear the music outside.

Walter says, "Don't take that sign too serious. Some of the kids in the Club are pretty tough. But when they get to doing real skating, artistic skating, they forget about fighting." He holds open the door. The music grabs you inside your chest and starts pumping all through your body. "That's disco,"

Walter says. "The session will be over at eight o'-clock, and then we have Club time with some real music."

We're inside this huge place; the end could be half a mile away. Diana Ross, the Beatles, Michael Jackson, in glitter paint, are twenty feet high on the sides. I'm watching the shiny wood floor whirling around under about a thousand roller skates, and I'm getting dizzy with the lights flaking off the turning mirrored balls, coming down like colored snow.

Walter steers me to the skate rental. "Fit this boy good, Charlie. He's going to be a fine skater. Yes, oh, yes." He's smiling all over. This Walter is one happy dude.

He helps me lace up right, feels for my toes through the boots, and spins the wheels with his thumb to see that they've got good action. I stand up and shove off into a rolling New Year's Eve party. I don't know how, but I got invited to the party too. I've skated before, with clamp-on skates in the street, so I stay up on my wheels O.K. Then the music starts flying me around. I'm flapping my arms, grinning and waving at Walter every time I come by. "Take it easy, hotshot," I tell myself, but I'm not listening. This is great!

The music is dying, and Walter's soft voice turns into thunder from the ceiling. He's talking into a mike. "Ladies and gentlemen, this session at the Roller Paradise Rink is over. Thank you for your attendance, and anybody who is in the Club can

41

stay for lessons." The thousand people start taking their skates off, leaving about twenty-five teenagers and Walter in the middle of the rink.

"Come on over here, Robert!" He waves me toward him. "This is Robert," he says, his arm around my shoulder. "And this is the Club: Kenny, Maurice, Shirley, Jerry, Phil, Linda, and etcetera. You won't remember all the names right away, but these are your skating buddies. Get to know 'em and they'll help you begin your career in artistic skating."

The way they're looking at me, I doubt it. Kenny flicks an eyelash toward me and goes into a twirl on two front wheels. Maurice grunts, like "Hi" is too much trouble. And Shirley looks me over, says, "Nice to meetcha, Robert," flips her little skirt, and takes off.

Linda knows she's cute—white skates, tan, smooth-stocking legs going up to meet a short, electric-blue outfit with zigzag sequins. Her eyes are outlined inky black, with shiny blue stuff smudged on the lids. They keep roaming under toothbrush lashes; she's got a radar fix on every guy on the rink. I know a girl in a Catholic-school uniform who's ten times cuter. *She's* beautiful.

Walter is showing Kenny how to come off a turn. "That's *real* good. You've got to end it good, too, like you were a star and those are your fans out there. You want to give 'em a show!" Walter goes into this fantastic spin. He comes out of it holding both arms high and proud toward the ghost fans he's seeing out there.

Kenny doesn't take it too well. "I coulda done it, but this crummy floor grabs my wheels."

"Yeah, Kenny, yeah," Maurice needles.

Walter's always patient. Most of the Club isn't like Kenny and Maurice. The others practice doing what Walter says without arguing or making wisecracks. Over and over they'll do a move, working around a circle on the floor, falling and getting up, and doing it again. Walter wants me to practice "stroking." That's using your legs to get power. Instead of clashing your wheels into the floor, you kind of glide each leg, bringing it up to the other one before you glide ahead again. Every time, you have to push hard with the back leg. And you're bending the knees but somehow holding your top part as if a broomstick is down your back.

"You're getting it, you're getting it!" Walter tells me. "Keep practicing." My legs are begging to quit, but I want to do this; I want to get powerful and swoop around the rink. Already I see myself zipping into "three-turns" and "Mohawks." Jerry takes time off from practicing advanced stuff to help me with my power push.

When the Club time is up, Jerry says, "Walter, give us an exhibition. Come on! We've got to have something to shoot for."

"Come on, Walter!" the Club yells.

Walter is shy but pleased. He puts on a tape. Rimsky-Korsakov is the name on the cassette. "It's classical," he explains to me.

Now, I can't believe what I see! This is Walter,

43

big, gray haired, gentle, a guy who's got hundreds of Twinkies stored around his middle. He's standing alone in the center of this huge floor, straight and serious and tall as a king! His head's up waiting for the tape. And when the music comes foaming down from the amps, he leans into the air. His legs go scissoring around the rink so fast, he shrinks it to a kiddy playground. He's playing with the music. He's forward; he's backward! He's running ahead of it and turning to let it catch him again.

Music like this I've never heard. It's got circuses, and cowboys; it shouts and laughs; it goes sad and quiet. And Walter is acting all that with his arms and his whole self.

Margaret Mary said he was a champion, and this must be "artistic skating." Could that ever be *me* out there? That's a laugh. He's spinning! His body's melting in the speed, but I can see his face. It's beautiful. Sort of religious, like he's praying. Like he can see right into Heaven! The music lifts into one big wave and crashes down. Walter's on one knee, arms up and back, bowing with his head low.

It's a minute before the Club can do anything. Then they start beating their hands and yelling, "All *right*, Walter!" Even Kenny's doing it.

"Oh, geez, I gotta work on my backward edges, and you gotta work on pushing with that free leg," Jerry says to me. "If we practice a thousand, thousand times, we'll make it." "We?" He's a nice guy, this Jerry.

Walter's perspiring and grunting when he bends

to take off his skates. I feel lucky and proud sitting next to him.

"Walter," I say, "it was so great the way you did that!" Maybe this is the first time I've talked right to him. He looks surprised.

"Oh, yes? Well, it's just the expression makes it look good."

"Night, Walter! See you next Thursday!" The Club kids its way through the big doors. "Quit it! Get your fat hands offa me, I said!" Linda's giving it to Maurice, but she bumps him going out.

We're walking home along the side of the park. "I wouldn't go through the park anymore at night," Walter says. "It's not like when I was a kid coming up. Our house was on Fourth Avenue, and my gang used to walk over to the rink through the park just about every day and stay maybe ten hours. In summer only, of course, account of school the rest of the time. I've been meaning to ask you, Robert. Err-uh, where do you go to school?"

"Well, I was staying all around, so I didn't get to go to any one school."

"Oh, I see, yes. After your mother died, I guess you went to be with different relations?"

"No, uh, it was really foster homes before she died. She really wanted to, uh, take care of me, but she was pretty young and sometimes she couldn't, apartment too crowded and stuff like that. So the court put me in foster homes."

"Well, they must've been good to you in the foster homes? The court wouldn't send you anyplace that

45

wasn't a good place, and people wouldn't want to be foster parents unless they really liked kids, now would they?"

There you go, Walter, thinking everybody's like you. Yeah, foster homes are real sweet places. You oughta been with me and Ronald and Reginald in the foster home in Bensonhurst. I was maybe ten. . . .

Ronald, he's small, juiced up, always talking big, dancing on his toes like a prizefighter, giving me these teasing little punches.

"Quit it, Ronald!"

"This place stinks!" he says, still dancing around. "Bensonhurst is for the birds. I'm gonna get me some action down at 42nd Street and Times Square!"

"The cops'll pick him up, won't they, Reggy?"

Reggy drags on his cigarette. "Whadda they gonna do, the cops? All over the city kids hookin' school. Whadda they gonna do to ya? Truant officer, what's he gonna do, call ya muthah? Ya muthah says, 'You find 'im, you can keep 'im.' "

Then Reggy hits twelve; he's not waiting anymore. He takes off. Foster mother's real mad— there goes $240 a month. "Why didn't you boys tell me?!" I'm not telling *anybody anything*. Reggy said he'd come back and push me under a bus if I did.

Even now, when I'm on the subway, I look at guys riding between the cars, swaying, hands in their pockets, sneakers braced, like they've gotta prove that *you're* scared to die, but *they're* not. I look to see if it's Reggy.

Walter's waiting for me to say something, but I'm

still in Bensonhurst. "And when you heard your mother passed away, you felt so bad you ran in the park, and that's where Margaret Mary found, err, met you?"

"Sort of, yeah."

"I know how you must've felt, Robert. When I was a little fellow, my mother used to carry me all those blocks over to Methodist Hospital. For my ear, you know. It got infected all the time. And we'd sit in the clinic and wait for maybe three hours, and I'd be crying, it hurt so bad. My mother never put me down for a minute. She'd rock me, and sometimes she'd sing this old song to try and make me laugh: 'Horsey, git your tail up, keep the sun outa my eyes!' "

I'm pretty quiet, so Walter says, "If you're interested, Robert, I could show you pictures and articles about the really great stars of artistic roller-skating."

"But how did *you* get to skate the way you do? I mean, with those motions and everything?"

"That's a long story. I don't know if you want to hear it."

"Oh, yeah!"

"Well, I must have been four years old; it was 1923 or '24 when my mother got me my first pair of skates. I can still smell the oil! They had straps then, and clamps, and red wheels. I loved those red wheels. I put 'em on in the backyard, where there's cement, you know. And the next thing, I'm street skating. Best thing, if you're a little squirt, just playing around on your wheels all day.

47

"About nine or ten I saw *Roller Vanities*. From then on, there was nothing else in the world for me. That freestyle, you know, everybody dressed up in fine costumes, just flying, flying!

"Then in my teens, I saw a great, great skater interpreting the 'Ave Maria.' It was a prayer on skates. Made you cry, it was so beautiful."

"That's the way *you* do it! Serious and sort of acting it. How did you learn to do that?"

"Now you've hit it! That's the artistic skating!" He's getting excited. "You don't 'learn' it. It's something you'll *feel*. Of course, some skaters never get that. Oh, they can do their Mohawks and Choctaws and spins good enough to pass all their tests. But it's only a few that *feel* it, and that makes them different. Audiences know which ones. They shout and cheer when they see them.

"Now, I think—yes, I really think you might be one of those different ones. You've got a nice line, hold yourself real straight. Most beginners, they bend over, straddle with their legs. We'll get you working the circles, finding your edges. Pretty soon you'll be as good as anybody in the Club. If you really want it enough to work and work and work some more, if you do, I could help you, train you."

He's waiting so hopefully for me to answer. He's expecting too much from me! I'd just mess up. "Fourteen's too old to start," I say. "It's already too late."

"No! My goodness, no! You could do it!"

"Thanks, I think I'll just come around the rink

48

once in a while, but not the other stuff." He looks so sad. I wish I could do what he wants, but I *can't*. Besides, what makes him so sure I'm even gonna be around?

Brooklyn's dark around us. No end to all the brownstone houses, just going, going, down to the black river. "Well." Walter clears his throat. "How about a cup of hot chocolate? Margaret Mary'll have some for us, you can bet."

We turn our corner, and the old gate is really mad at being waked up. Down at the end of the path, in a square of yellow light cut out of the dark, Margaret Mary's waiting. Heather-Belle and Big Boy, too.

5

At breakfast I'm facing the ol' oatmeal again. Luckily there's a Danish, too, and I'm taking bites to help the gray stuff go down. Margaret Mary thinks oatmeal gives you strength. "The Scottish people have been eating it for hundreds of years," she says. "And I never saw a Scotsman who wasn't strong."

Walter's gone to work. All night I've been sweating this dream about him. Walter's giving me a present, a birthday present, I think. And I kick it out of his hand. His face looks like he's going to cry.

"Walter told me to tell you where the newspaper depot is. It's down 15th Street to Fourth Avenue, turn right, and there'll be a boarded-up store. There's a door in the boards, and Mr. Pomerantz is inside. He buys the newspapers. Oh, Walter says he saw a supermarket shopping cart in the bushes at that vacant lot a couple of doors down, if it's still there. He'll help you fix it so it goes good. And he left these magazines for you to look at. They're all about skating. I wish he had the picture of himself when he was the gold-medal champion. He was such a beautiful skater! We had a fire once, only a small one, and darned if *those* pictures didn't get burned up."

The pages are yellow and flaky. Walter's been saving them since the thirties. Here's a guy with black, tight trousers and sequins all over his shirt, moving up into the air, arms out, reaching for some wonderful thing. Under the picture it says, "A Nijinsky on Wheels."

"That's Gloria Nord." Margaret Mary points to another picture. "I saw her at the Roller-Drome when Walter took me. Oh, she was a pretty little thing, all white and pink and gold—like a doll you win at the carnival."

"I think I better go now, to the newspaper place I mean."

"Oh, just a minute . . ." Margaret Mary opens another of her Zippy Supermarket bags and takes out a sweater. "Now, I don't know if you like navy blue, but I saw this at the Second Chance clothing store down here on Fifth Avenue, and I thought, 'Robert would look so good in this!' It's almost new; they didn't have any other colors . . ." She's getting nervous.

I can't say anything, but not because it's navy; it's

51

because they're so nice to me, Margaret Mary and Walter. The shouldn't be doing all this for some bozo like me!

"That's real fine," I manage, and I reach out to touch it.

"Go ahead! Put it on!" She's smiling again. "There's pretty blue pants there too, but you'd have to try them on. Oh, I guessed the size, and I was right! You look grand! That's what my dad used to say when one of us was all dressed up. We had seven in the family, you know. It was quite a sight, all of us on a Sunday!"

I just stand there, stroking the soft wool. Then she's pushing me into the hall where there's an old, blurred mirror. Everything it ever saw is still in there, out of focus. But I can make out this dude looking sideways at himself. "You know, you don't look half bad. Dawn Marie might even go out on a date with you." Then I scratch that idea. Sure. After I get through picking old newspapers out of the trash, she'd *love* to go out with me!

"I'll save the sweater for special," I tell Margaret Mary, who's flittering around me, looking happy. "It's a beauty. But my old one's good enough for work. I better get going."

"Here," she says. "Here's a sandwich for lunch, the same kind I gave to Walter, Muenster cheese." She shoves this little bag at me, and I head out the door.

Heather-Belle rolls down the walk, keeping me company. The old gate sighs open and I'm on the

52

street, beginning my new career: trash man.

"Well, Paul, ol' buddy, sometimes there's things us guys gotta do, make a living and all that stuff."

"Yeah, Robert." Paul Newman grins. "At least you'll get plenty of fresh air."

Marsha's on her front steps, singing into her telephone. When she sees me, she waves both her hands. "Hey! Robert! Hey!" like I was the president, or a movie star come to Brooklyn. I don't know—do people like Marsha have favorite movie stars? Mickey Mouse would be hers, I guess.

"Hi, Marsha. How you doing today?" She grins and grins. "Well, it's nice talking to you. Take care, Marsha," and I start trotting slantways across Seventh Avenue to save time. "Cross at the corner, you Robert!" she yells, getting all excited. So I backtrack and wait for the light at the corner. She's watching me. "Walk! It says 'Walk'! Now you cross!"

The shopping cart is where Walter said, turned over in the bushes, and it's wobbly but O.K. Well, there's nothing to do but start pushing. So here I am going up and down the streets, poking in the stuff that's set out for the garbage truck. At first I feel everybody's looking, that they're going to say, "Whatcha doin' there, boy?!" as if I was stealing something valuable.

Then I get used to it. Nobody sees me, nobody cares any more than they ever did. And I'm piling up stacks of papers, higher and higher, in the cart. Doesn't take much of your mind to do it, so I'm gazing down the endless brownstone fronts, the empty, gray-stick trees, all the way to the black, oily Gowanus Canal. Wait . . . in the little squares of dirt they have in front of all the brownstones, tiny flags are sticking up: purple, green, and white. It's a little parade of flowers. Even in Brooklyn!

I'm nervous when a blue-and-white police car shoots out of 5th Street. The two heads inside are talking, but their eyes are sweeping the neighborhood like searchlights. It's O.K. They check me out and go back to deciding, will it be the deli or McDonald's for lunch? I'm big enough to be sixteen. They probably figure I quit school to go to work.

On Seventh Avenue, where the stores are, you see these hippie girls hurrying along. Maybe they're ladies, but you can't tell how old they are. They've got frizzy hairdos, Mexican ponchos, and big, over-the-shoulder bags, on top of pink Adidas. And the guys are young and getting bald, with little backpacks and scared looks. Maybe they're scared of the pink Adidas girls?

My adrenalin starts pumping. Ahead of me, near the high school, there's a woman walking. Is it my mother?! Her hair is down her back like a jungle girl's. Her jeans fit too good, and she's got these heels that could stab you through the heart. Her blouse is so red, with piles of red ruffles, you could see it from Flatbush Avenue. And when she turns her head to look in the window of a ladies' underwear store, her lips are pouting and her pretty face—well, once it was pretty—is angry at everything. But it's cool—she's not my mother. Nostrand Avenue is too far away for her to be coming over here.

Angry, always angry, my mother. I remember we're standing in Coney Island Amusement Park with all the light bulbs in dots around everything, and outside the park is black night. My mother's angry face is bending over me, and she's smoking her cigarette hard. She yanks my shirt down and smears a rough paper napkin across my face. "Do you have to eat so disgusting?!"

The roller-coaster is making its terrible diving noise right on top of us, and the man is shouting, "Hurry! Hurry! See the alligator-boy! He's got bumps on his skin like a alligator, folks, and frog's webs between his toes! Step right up! The show is going on right now! Hurry! Hurry!" What did he do, that alligator-boy, to get to look like that picture? Did he suck his thumb? Maybe he wet his pants.

The teenage girls and their boyfriends are screaming and laughing on the rides. She's mad because they can do whatever they want. Here she's got all this pretty lipstick, and black mascara eyes, high heels, a red ruffle blouse over Lee Riders, and she's stuck with a little kid hanging on her. Sometimes she looks like *she's* the little kid and it's a big mistake—"Who is this pain-in-a-neck kid always follow-in' me? I wanna have fun! How can I have fun if this little kid is draggin' on me?"

But when I was real small, I couldn't help it. I was always reaching to touch her and hold on to her, and that made her madder. After the judge said, "This child is a juvenile in need of supervision," and they started putting me in the foster homes, I got better at not bothering her. I mean, when the caseworker brought her to visit, I knew not to climb on her and muss her blouse.

You learn, after a while you learn, how to make it. *Don't snivel*, and don't expect *nothin'* from *nobody*. Even if they want to do something nice for you, help you out a little, they got their own selves to worry about. "Sorry, Robert, you got to go here. You can't stay there, because The Law says so. You'll see; it's really better for you."

Yeah, tell me about it. I used to let it get to me, but now I just play it c-o-ol, like my ol' buddy Paul.

Margaret Mary and Walter may be throwing me a curve. Caseworker didn't give them money to buy that sweater. I haven't got them figured out yet. But, hey, why not stick around as long as it lasts? If they wanna be suckers, I didn't ask 'em to, now did I?

Turning up 1st Street I see another cart, toppling over with newspapers. It's being pushed, you can't see by who, he's so bent over. It's a man, but a shrunken man. His head is down low, except when he ducks it around to look out for cars. Then I see his face. He's shriveled like an old balloon. I see his blue, nowhere eyes. Is he sore that I'm coming into his territory? He's not mad *or* sad. He goes on pushing like he's been pushing since he's five years old and his hands grew to the shopping cart. I haul out of there, get off this street fast. You feel *bad* to see somebody like that.

We, this cart and me, seem to be steering toward Eighth Avenue and 6th Street—St. Saviour's High School. Why am I doing this? What if she just happened to be looking out the window?! I spin that cart around, taking the curve like the Indy 500, and I'm safe on 5th Street going up toward the park.

Not many newspapers along Prospect Park West. So I sit on a bench for a few minutes. There's a lot of graffiti: TERRY LOVES DEE-DEE 4EVER, TYRONE THE BEST, SCHOOL STINKS!, etc. I've got this Magic Marker somebody threw away, but there's still some color in it. I write ROBERT AND DAWN MARIE 4EVER way on the side of the bench where you'd never notice.

The newspapers are so high and heavy now, I figure it's time to find Mr. Pomerantz. I get myself moving: Seventh, Sixth, Fifth, Fourth. From here, looking down to 9th street, you see a concrete monster spraddling its legs over the streets. It's a robot grasshopper, bending over so the F train can run on its back to Manhattan. I push along 'til I'm under it.

The houses under here are little dark-red and dark-gray boxes, shaking when the F train roars on top of them. It's not much of a neighborhood, mostly cars going over on the expressway. And the few cars hurrying down in the streets, seems like the people in them are afraid the bashed tin cans, and smashed bottles, and broken truck bodies, are going to grab them going by.

Mr. Pomerantz is where Walter said he'd be, under

the expressway, in back of the boarded-up store. It's dark in there; then a darker spot moves. It's Mr. Pomerantz. He's all over gray, like the pollution from the expressway's been dusting down on him for fifty years. He takes my newspapers, weighs them, and gives me the change. It isn't much, but that's what they pay. "Hey, Mr. Pomerantz!" I want to say when I'm leaving. "It's almost spring! You don't want to stay inside all the time." But I don't.

"Frankeee! Gimme a bite a ya crummy pizza!" Gold metallic jackets, red jellies so pointy they could spear you, fake-fur collars on aviator jackets flipped up in back of the guys' heads, cherry-candy lips popping bubble gum, and blue plastic earrings hanging three inches down. This guy's walking tight with his girlfriend, and three other chicks are eye-balling them. Two thousand pairs of jeans on the sidewalk, so tight kids have to lie down on the bed to zip them up. John Jay, the big high school on Seventh Avenue, is letting out for lunch. If I hustle, I could just happen to be going by St. Saviour's when Dawn Marie comes out for lunch. You knew that's where you were going anyway, Slim.

The teenagers are busting out, laughing and shrieking and kidding each other. They're all around me and my cart. I could be a tree or a stone, but that's O.K. Then, a block away, I see a little lady walking along. She's holding a kid by the hand who's much bigger than she is. They're walking slow because the kid's feet turn out sideways in big policeman's shoes. It's Mrs. Polini and Marsha.

When Marsha sees me, she's going to start screaming, and these John Jay kids will be looking at me—"Dig this guy! He's got a ree-tard for a girlfriend." I could pretend I don't see them, put my head down and make a run for the parking lot. But hell, that'd hurt Mrs. Polini. And besides, Marsha's got a right to have friends, even if she's not wearing pointy pink shoes. So I push ahead to meet them.

"Robert!!" Marsha lets out a blast. Then she starts moaning and trying to put her head on my shoulder, she's so happy. Mrs. Polini is pulling her back, but Marsha's much stronger.

"That's not nice, Marsha! I'm sorry, Robert!"

"That's all right, Mrs. Polini. How you doin', Marsha? Did you go shopping?"

"I went to the store and the man gave me baloney, yes. You could have it, Robert." She takes out this piece of baloney from a little paper bag she's carrying.

I say, "Thanks, Marsha, but I got my sandwich. See. Margaret Mary made it for me, and she'd be sad if I didn't eat it."

"She can't help it, Robert. She likes people so much." Mrs. Polini is still apologizing. The John Jay kids aren't even noticing us. I'm glancing up the block and I see . . . Oh, no! I see *her* walking, holding her books in her arms. Only it's not walking. It's prettier than that. Her head's up, and her hair is floating, and her shoes barely touch the ground.

59

I want to ditch the wagon and the few papers I picked up and run! It's too late. She's coming toward us. Oh, fine, fine! Now she knows I'm a trash peddler. Dawn Marie chats with Mrs. Polini and Marsha. Then she says, "Take care, Mrs. Polini. 'Bye, Marsha." And somehow we're walking along together. "I'm going to my girl friend Nadine's house, on 10th Street," she says.

One of her books slides off and falls. I pick it up for her. "Oh, thank you. That's my history book. Do you like history?" I shrug my shoulders. History is something I never think much about. "Some kids say it's boring, but I like it. All those people . . . I mean, they've been here on the earth, and now they're gone. I like to read about it; it's sad, but nice." She begins to turn pink, like maybe I'll laugh at her.

Quickly, I say, "Yeah, I know what you mean. At the school where I went, we had all that stuff about the Civil War, and, you know, Pilgrims. Those Pilgrims, I never liked 'em—a bunch of mean dudes. But for the Civil War we had a teacher who took us to see *Gone with the Wind*. They burned up the whole city, and this woman had to eat dirt, she was so hungry." I start getting nervous here. Maybe Dawn Marie will think I'm trying to bring up those love scenes.

"Oh, yes!" she says. "And the little girl, Bonnie Blue, jumped with that pony and broke her neck! That was so sad!"

By now I'm not even worrying what she'll think

of my "work." "Here, why don't you put your books in the cart. I'll carry them for you." She puts them on top of the few papers I picked up coming from Mr. Pomerantz's.

"Do you get a lot of papers? I mean so you can make enough money?"

"Well, I guess everybody in Brooklyn reads the *Post* or the *News*. Around here, they get the *Times*, too. That's good, because on Sunday you wouldn't believe how thick it is. But they don't pay too much for a stack way over the top of this cart. You've got to hustle to get any kind of money." I don't tell her how little that is. "I want to help out Margaret Mary and Walter. They've been so nice to me." She nods.

What else can we talk about? I could talk with her forever. We're passing St. Saviour's Church, which is not exactly in Nadine's direction, but we seem to be taking the long way around.

There's a funeral going on. When I was little, lookng out of Auntie Alice's window, I didn't know what was in the long boxes. Now I do, and it gives me a weird feeling. I'm not scared of the dead person so much. It's those guys in the black suits— they're smoking and looking all around like it's a bore, this person being dead.

"Do you think there's a Heaven, or anything, to go to when you die?" I ask her.

"I think there *is* a Heaven but not a Hell. God wouldn't be so mean. Sister Mary Agnes—that's our athletic coach and everybody likes her—she's sure it's there. But she wouldn't know what to do in

61

Heaven, she says. She'd rather be busy down here, refereeing girls' basketball and playing with her nieces and nephews when she goes home. And my mother always says she'll know she's in Heaven when there's a washer and dryer on the premises, and nobody has to drag their shopping carts to the Laundromat anymore."

"But how do you *know*?"

Dawn Marie looks very serious. "Well, my grandmother died. And I know she's in Heaven because she was so good to me. She didn't speak English very well, but she'd tell me all about how it was in Italy when she was a girl. And there was a certain kind of little, sweet biscuit, and she'd always get them from the Italian bakery just for me. We're Italian, you know." She looks at me as if she's worrying that maybe this might make a difference.

"Oh, I know!" (Her last name is Di Falco. I happened to ask Margaret Mary.) "It must be neat to be Italian, or Irish, or something. You get to hear all those stories about the old days."

"Yes." She smiles. "They used to have dances in the little town she came from, and the girls wore these big, whirly skirts. At the dances, I mean. And there were real fruit trees everywhere, all white in the springtime.

"Since I was very little, I went to her house. My mother worked till my father got the insurance agency—he's the agent for the whole Park Slope, for Eagle Guaranteed Claims Company. Then she could stay home. But I still ran over to Nonna's all the time. She never talked bad about anybody on the block. She was always helping them. And she got me my first heels—little blue ones with a T strap. She couldn't be just gone. I feel that she's up there, somewhere beautiful—like Italy."

Dawn Marie, for you and Margaret Mary and Walter *and* your grandmother, there's got to be a Heaven. For the rest of us, forget it! Anyway, who cares? I'm in Heaven right now, talking to you.

We're at her girl friend's apartment house now. "Well, uh," I say. And she says, "Well, um," at the very same moment. We laugh about that. Then Dawn Marie picks up her books from the wagon.

"I have so much French homework, and tests tomorrow. I've got to go." And she runs up the steps so light, that dancing way. I want to run up too, like Gene Kelly in *Singin' in the Rain*, and tap-dance her right down the steps and away.

At the big glass door she turns for a minute. I'm pushing off, and I turn too. Then the door closes.

What is this? Am I going crazy or something? Did it really happen that we walked in the street together and she wasn't ashamed for people to see her with me? Maybe some junkie stuck a needle in that Danish this morning. That's it: I'm on drugs; I'm dreaming!

The old gate chuckles open. Heather-Belle comes wheezing and smiling down the walk for a chin scratch. Nobody seems to be home, but stuck on the fridge is a note. *Dear Robert, I've gone to feed the dogs in the park. A jelly doughnut is in the bread box. Margaret Mary.* There's a scribbled-over word before the name that looks like Mom, but it couldn't be. I'm just dreaming again.

6

Couple of days later, I'm sitting on the wall with a custard doughnut in my hand. Heather's looking up at me. "Who do you love, me or the doughnut? Don't answer that!"

Heather says, "Both." She gets a piece even though she's too fat.

"You sure get happy easy, Heather-Belle. A piece of a doughnut and a chin scratch is all it takes."

Holding what's left of the doughnut in my hand, I'm ready for some heavy-duty dreaming. . . . What if, just what if I ever got the nerve to ask Dawn Marie for a date? How many newspapers before I save enough money? Not that she'd be the kind you have to spend big money on, but I figure on giving Margaret Mary and Walter most of what I make. How much would I need to take her to Manhattan on a date? Of course we'd go to Manhattan. Brooklyn's too old and ugly for Dawn Marie. She wouldn't go with me, but listen, anybody's allowed to dream.

The mirror's got a picture coming up on its cracked, old, cloudy face. It's me, wearing a cool maroon sweater, and brand-new loafers with a gold buckle and a soft shine. I turn, checking out how the tan slacks flare over the backs of my loafers. Slacks have got to almost, but not quite, touch the ground.

Margaret Mary and Walter are in the mirror, too. They're offering me one of Walter's neckties from thirty years ago. "I don't think they wear ties anymore on a date, but thanks anyway."

"Have a good time!" Margaret Mary says, and Walter pulls me to the side.

"If you need any money, Robert—?" He's reaching for his wallet, but I gently push it back in his pocket and show him the twenty dollars in mine.

"Have a good time!" Margaret Mary says again, as I'm going out the door.

I'm walking along, listening to my new leather meeting the pavement. It's a cool sound, like a man taking his time but going somewhere important. Maybe he's reaching for his keys that fit in the side of a white Mercedes. Hey! The only Mercedes you've got is a shopping cart! Slow down, Slim! So what? Doesn't bother me. Nothing both ers me. I take off into the air like "Nijinsky on Wheels." Anybody watching? Who cares? I'm going out on a date with Dawn Marie!

What will she be wearing? Blue, I think, but not navy. A kind of straight blue coat, and she'll have a little pocketbook on a gold chain hanging from her hand. And stockings, not those dark-green knee-his. Maybe shiny black shoes with little heels.

I'm punching the doorbell. Her mother comes to the door. "Oh, here's that nice boy, Robert." (I can't get the mother in focus because I've never seen her, but let's say she says that.) "Dawn M'ree! Robert's here!"

I look up and she's coming down the stairs. I don't notice *what* she's wearing. She's smiling straight at me, like I'm the guy she's been waiting for all her life. I'm knocked out, but I manage to say good-bye to her mother, and promise we won't be home late from Manhattan.

We walk along sort of carefully on account of our clothes. "You look really nice, Robert."

I'm supposed to say that to her first! I swallow hard. "You look beautiful." She blushes. Then I say, "I guess you've been to Manhattan a lot?"

"No—my parents were born here in Brooklyn, in the neighborhood, and they don't like New York too much."

"I thought we'd take the F train in and maybe

get off at Rockefeller Center. There's a skating rink right on the bottom of these giant skyscrapers. People can watch for free." Oh geez, she's going to think I don't want to spend money on her! "I mean, after that, we can get something to eat, even go to a movie, if you'd like."

"It doesn't matter." She smiles.

We're going down the subway stairs, and I think I ought to kind of steer her arm—I've seen guys do that. But she might think I was trying to make a move on her. When I push my twenty dollars under the glass window, I start worrying. There's $2.00 gone. And another $2.00 for the way home. Geez! Suppose she says she wants to go to Radio City Music Hall or something?

"Are you warm enough? It's so cold down here in the subway, you'd think they've got a special machine for making it cold."

She shakes her head. "This is my good coat, and it's really warm." The platform is trembling; that means the F train's chewing up the tracks between Coney Island and here. The purple-and-white F on its face glares at us. It's coming on fast, banging from side to side and roaring like it's chained and it's mad. I move in front of Dawn Marie in case some maniac might be thinking of pushing her onto the track. He'd have to kill me first!

"Where would you like to sit?" First we try the two-seaters facing backward. Then we jump up and go for ones where we can see out the window better. After Seventh Avenue it's crazy. The subway goes outside and you shoot into a purple sky, streaked red and orange and green from Jersey to Canarsie. The whole of Brooklyn is tilting under you. I used to have to go with my mother to the city. She needed me to carry the kid while she shopped on 14th Street. And I loved this part.

"Dawn Marie! There's the Statue of Liberty!"

"Where?! Oh, I see it! I haven't been there yet. When my uncle came from Jersey we were going, but it snowed."

"I'll take you sometime," I tell her. "That city, hanging in the air, that's Manhattan."

"It looks like it's so far away, we could never get there," she says.

Now the tunnel swallows our car into the dark. We sit back and watch the people. But I start watching her. "I knew you'd have a blue coat," I tell her. And sure enough, she's got patent-leather pumps with little heels she keeps on the floor pointing straight in front of her.

"Your sweater is pretty," she says. "Maroon is my favorite color for a boy's sweater."

"Mine too. That's a pretty smell on you. What is it, tulips or something?"

69

"Oh, it's Eau de Fleur toilet water. That's a French name," she says.

"It's wonderful how you can say it. It sounds like real French."

She goes pink. "I take French at St. Saviour's. That's how I know how to say it. Otherwise I wouldn't ever, because French doesn't sound the way it looks. I get terrible marks, but I still love it."

We're quiet for a while. That's not because we don't know what to say, but because it's just good being quiet together.

When the train stops at 50th Street, we get off. Now it's New York City—quick people moving, moving everywhere. "This is it, the Big Apple," I tell her. And I stay close so nobody bumps into her. When we come out of the ground, we stand with our heads way back. The long, long lit-up buildings sway over us, and the sky is deep purple with a few white stars. Lights, lights everywhere, enough to be Christmas. I sneak a look at Dawn Marie. She reminds me of a little kid I saw near A&S last Christmas, gazing at the lights. She has the same kind of Christmas face.

"Is that Radio City Music Hall?"

Like a fool I say, "Do you want to see what show they have?" We're looking past these important door captains into this giant, slick, curvy lobby. With all the buttons, these guys look like cash registers. On the walls are photos of all the movie stars. I'm praying she doesn't want to go in and see the show. One ticket is more than ten dollars!

"It's really pretty," she says. "Let's go see the skating rink."

We're running down the block, laughing and laughing, all out of breath, until we see this enormous golden man who swims sideways over the rink. He'd make a terrific radiator cap on a 1940 Buick. Flags are slapping the breeze on poles around the rink, and we put our elbows on the marble wall to look down.

"It's small, isn't it?" she says. "It's like a postcard picture and we're looking down into it."

"See, Dawn Marie, when that guy turns, he leans just a little bit. That's how he can do it. If he stayed flat on his blades, he'd never make it. He's got to go on the edges. Walter taught me that."

She's interested in how the girls do their arms.

"Isn't that one wonderful? She's like a ballerina. I took ballet when I was nine years old. I loved it, but it got too expensive." For about an hour we watch, feeling almost like we're gliding and turning too.

"Say, how would you like something to eat? If you're hungry, we could maybe get a pizza. Or frozen custard. Or whatever you like."

She smiles. "Pizza's fine."

"And we can get frozen custard after." I touch her arm just enough to steer her to Sixth Avenue and 42nd, where there's a pizza place.

The guy behind the counter is Greek. His store has souvlaki, pizza, and egg rolls. He's twirling the circle of dough and singing like it's an opera, which makes Dawn Marie laugh. We get two slices and carry them to this little table. I wipe her chair off good with a paper napkin and we sit down.

"Pizza's my favorite food, I mean restaurant food. Margaret Mary cooks very good, but she doesn't make pizza. Here, do you want some extra cheese, or garlic and red pepper? Is yours good?"

"It really is. This is probably the best crust I ever had."

"I'm glad."

She eats so pretty and neat. I hope I'm not making disgusting noises!

"Thank you. It was really good," she says to the pizza store man when we leave. A couple of stores down, there's a frozen custard place.

"Give us two one-dollar cones, please. Do you like chocolate or vanilla, Dawn Marie?" (I say her name as much as I can.) We both take vanilla. It comes squeezing out of the machine like toothpaste, and the girl gets under the smooth ribbon with the cone and catches it into a white mountain with a curled-over point.

72

"I always eat the point first," Dawn Marie says.

"That's funny! Me too!"

We're strolling across on 42nd toward the library. "I've had frozen custard all over this whole city practically, and they have the best. I'm glad I didn't get chocolate."

"Vanilla is the best flavor," she agrees.

Dawn Marie's so pleased at the lions. "They've seen history go right in front of them. I mean, there were ladies in skirts that came down to the sidewalk, and little hats with birds, and men with those round derbies. Everybody went in horse carriages then, instead of cars."

We walk and walk. This funny, high old building is sailing right toward us at 23rd Street. Dawn Marie says, "On T.V. I saw an old newsreel picture of ocean liners they used to have in the Hudson River. That building looks like one of them, sailing on the river, doesn't it?"

"That's just what I was thinking!" I love that we have the same thoughts.

We must have walked fifty blocks and I could keep on walking, to Chinatown, to the East River, and never get tired. "Oh, gee, you're not tired, are you, Dawn Marie?"

"Not a bit. I love to walk." She doesn't say "with *you*," but maybe she almost did.

When we get to Washington Square Park, she says, "It must be close to nine o'clock. My mother

73

will be upset if we're not home by ten."

"O.K., we'll just get on the subway at West 4th Street." On the train we sit very straight, but I can feel her sleeve warm against mine. If only she'd put her hand on my hand the way that says, "This is my boyfriend. I'm his girlfriend." But that's dreaming *too* much.

Heather-Belle's licking the doughnut in my hand, and Margaret Mary's squeaking open the gate. Time to wake up, Slim.

7

It's Friday afternoon. This week screeched by like *Road Runner*. Wish I could turn a handle and run it backward. Every time Walter'd try to walk in the door at the police station, I'd crank him right out again. And the three of us could just keep doing all the dumb, nice things they do around here.

I'm coming in at the door thinking, "Robert, you've had it. It's time to split." Except I don't know where I'm going, exactly. Margaret Mary's sitting at the kitchen table with her back to me. Her hat is knocked over sideways on her head and she's sort of slumped down like the air's been pumped out of her. Must have gotten the news about me having to go, because it's not like Margaret Mary to be just sitting. Usually, if she's not rescuing cats or squirrels, she's out visiting all these old losers up and down the street or over by the park. Even the snooty ones

75

like Gloria who think they're better than Margaret Mary, she's always helping them, too.

A few days ago she's trying free makeup samples they were handing out at Woolworth's. "Which lipstick do you think looks good on me? This pink one or this purpley one?" And Walter says, "That one. That color looks real pretty on you." And he means it! They're two old nuts, but I'm gonna miss 'em.

When she hears me and turns around, I see her eyes are all red. Right away she says, "Just a little congestion in the eyes, you know. It's nothing. Best thing is just keep busy and forget about it."

"Can I get you something at the drugstore? I can shop and cook supper, if you want," I tell her. She looks so sad, I'm feeling that grab in the chest that I don't want to feel. I'm only going to be saying "Good-bye," so why bother getting mixed up with these people?

Walter ducks his head in the doorway, looks at me and her, and says, "Now, honey, no need to, err-uh, worry about anything. Come on now." He's patting her. "Oh, you know that fellow Al, at the electric office? I was by there. Darned if he hasn't gone and gotten his shift changed this week! I won't be able to go down there again till my day off, *next* Friday."

You never saw "congestion" get cured so fast! She's practically skipping around the kitchen till bedtime. I'm going up the stairs telling myself, "Man!

It was pretty hairy there for a while, but if they want to play dumb games, it's all right with me."

Rain was tap-dancing on the roof all night. I poke my head out the window into the morning air. It's like a cool drink of water on my skin. Birds are yelling the news to each other, all at the same time, in every bush. Little brown Brooklyn birds, same color as the houses.

Walter's gray curls with the pink bald spot come under the window. Don't often see *that*, he's so tall. He's bending with a lot of sighs, picking something up out of the dirt and putting it into a can. Like he feels my eyes, he looks up smiling.

"Worms, Robert. I'm getting worms. They come out after the rain, you know." The look on my face says, "What the blankety-blank for?" "Fishing. They're the best for fishing. Beats all those shiny metal gidgets. Oh, I'm not going fishing, but some of the fellows are going down to Sheepshead Bay out on the party boats. They're taking flounder right about now in the bay, and living in apartments like they do, most of my friends don't get a chance to pick up many worms."

"I'm coming down!"

When I hit the garden, the sun is roaring up over Prospect Park. The light's surprising every piece of grass, every stick and bush. Walter holds out the can, and I look in at the pink, creepy mess.

"Now, Margaret Mary doesn't exactly like the idea

of feeding these little fellows to the fishes. But I figure as long as people are going to eat what they catch, there's no harm in it. We do eat hamburgers, you know."

I start hunting too. There's one out walking by the snowball bush. He's got all these pink elastic rings, and they keep squeezing and unsqueezing to get him where he wants to go. Grabbing a worm is a little weird. You dive down on him, but when you feel the moving between your two fingers, you want to drop him fast!

"Did you use to go fishing, Walter?"

"Oh, my, yes. We'd get up at four-thirty, and by five-fifteen we'd be on the subway with all our tackle and lunch. Quite a few beers in the cooler, too, of course. Then we'd be out on the jetty throwing our lines by six. All that nice fresh air and no crowds on the beach. It was mighty nice. If we caught something or not, didn't seem to matter. All of us joking around, pulling on the other guy's line so he'd think it was a fish! It was a lot of fun, I can tell you. Then, coming back on the subway, beer all gone and fish in the cooler, red as broiled lobsters every one of us, we'd be thinking we were heroes just for catching a few fish.

"That was before World War II. After, it wasn't the same. Things changed. Some of the fellows didn't come back, you know. The rest of us married with jobs and, err-uh, responsibilities." (I think he means kids, but him and Margaret Mary never talk about that.)

78

"Why don't you go now, if your friends are going?"

"Well, with my job, the way the hours are at the restaurant and all, it just doesn't seem to work out. Here, I guess we've got enough worms now. We'll put some of this wet grass on top of 'em, keep 'em cool and comfortable. Now I'll go in, get the coffee started, go pick up my paper."

"I'll go get it for you."

"No need, Robert. Why don't you just stay here and enjoy the nice morning? That way I get to see some of my buddies down at Tony's."

Something is floating around in my mind, a dead thing in the water I don't want to look at. The worms make me remember.

"Get it! Kill that sucker! Ooh-ee!" Melvin's sneaker comes down on this stupid worm. I mean, doesn't it know it's living on the grounds at Woodland Hall? It shoulda known it would get stomped by one of the "residents." And the butterflies ought to've learned it too. But they never do—just go flitterin' around like they were ladies in a shopping mall, looking at this, looking at that, sitting down for a minute to rest, and *wham!* Melvin or Ernie or Tyrone bashes 'em to the ground. Squirrels, teeny snakes, anything that's small and moves kind of fast, they've got to kill it. Maybe they're just not used to all this nature. But I think they're really scared that the squirrels

79

and snakes and moths and things are gonna attack and bite them to death.

I wish I could put up a sign on the high barbed wire fence: *"Don't* Come In Here, Birds, Squirrels, ETC.!" And have a skeleton's head with black holes for eyes on the bottom.

Our cottage is on a "hike" around Woodland Hall. The housemother and the social worker are always arranging dumb things like that. If they think Geronimo and Melvin and Tyrone and Ernie want to be Boy Scouts, they're loony; *they* need the counseling!

When we're out of sight of the main building, we throw these cheap little orange knapsacks down. They must have bought them at Lamston's for little Head Start kids. Melvin stretches out under a tree and pulls a cigarette out of his cap. Geronimo stands, leaning back on the tree, but his eyes aren't resting, they're everywhere like he's the lookout back at his clubhouse in New York City.

They're always talking about their clubs in the city. "Look at this crap we gotta wear," Melvin says. It's jeans and a white T-shirt. "Oh, God, if you coulda seen our club outfits! Every guy's got a club jacket, leather, with 'East New York Cobras' on the back. Black gloves with spikes we got, and motorcycle boots. And mirror shades that you can't see the eyes. Scare the mess outa any punk comes over on our streets."

Melvin's eleven like me. I think he was just in the club's junior divison. Didn't wear any of that stuff at all. Geronimo's cool. He's fourteen, and his club's the Knights of Death out in Queens. You can see him, all in black biker gear, and *nobody's* walking into *his* territory.

"Help! Oh, Mama, help!" James is screaming because a bee's fooling around his head. Everybody starts laughing. James is the youngest. He's always crying about something, and that's one thing you don't want to be doing around here. You've got to be BIG and BAD. Then the bee stings Melvin! What a gas! Melvin's screaming and running all around.

"Go git him, bee!" Ernie's glad to see Melvin get it; Melvin's always acting like the boss.

Geronimo says, "Come on. We got to finish this hike so we can get back."

I know what Geronimo's thinking. He wants to get to the magazines stashed in his mattress. That's all these guys want to do—stare at these crazy people-with-no-clothes-on pictures. Except James and me. We're noodling along, liking being out with the trees, finding little things down in the grass. James forgets he was crying and flops down into the green rug stuff they got all over the rocks out here.

"Look!" he says. "Lookit this bug!" He sticks

it gently with a piece of grass. This weird little beetle, or whatever, is nosing along with a T.V. antenna on his head. It's got a shiny shell with a green-and-gold finish like the Spanish guys' hot rods on Third Avenue. "Where you goin', huh? You want somethin' to eat? Here." James crumbles up some grass in front of it. The bug stumbles. He's trying to get somewhere, and we let him go.

"Robert, catch that worm on the walk there!"

"What for?"

"I want you should catch him and put him over in those leaves there. Then when they come back, Melvin wouldn't be able to step on him."

"Why don't you do it?" But I know he's a little scared to touch the worm, 'cause I am too. Is it gonna feel disgusting? Will it bite? Once I've got it by the tail, it's nothing. It's kind of pitiful, wanting to get away from the big giant, *me*. So we carry it over to a bunch of leaves and hide it way off the path.

They're coming, and we tag on behind, heading back to Maple Cottage. (There's Oak and Pine and Chestnut, too.) It's a real house, which is pretty nice compared to some of the holes I've been stuck in. Each cottage is supposed to be a "family"—ha, ha! James and me and Ernie, we're just PINS (that's Persons In Need of Supervision). But Tyrone and Melvin and Geronimo,

82

they're big-time operators. Melvin got arrested for carrying a gun to class at his school. Geronimo stole cars and beat up his girlfriend. Why would anybody do that to his girlfriend? And Tyrone's always running away from wherever they put him.

We stomp up the steps and the housemother looks like "Oh, Lord, they're back." She gets out of the hammock. "Put your stuff away where it belongs. Then you can watch T.V. till supper." Mrs. Dawkins isn't mean. It's just like she always says, "For what they're paying me, I don't need this aggravation."

Piling into the recreation room, Melvin and Geronimo get the best chairs, the big fat ones you fall down into. No question about it—they're the top dudes. Relaxing back, Melvin sticks out his foot so James falls over it.

"Oh, geez, don't cry, James. He'll just do it more," I say inside. And this time he doesn't. Tyrone flips on the T.V. and starts twirling the knob.

"Put on *Tom and Jerry*," Melvin tells him. Geronimo leans forward and switches to *The Dukes of Hazzard. No* argument. Around here what Geronimo wants, he gets, and he doesn't have to say a word.

We're all watching, looking like those guys coming across the field in *Night of the Living Dead*.

You just want to get in there, inside the screen with *Tom and Jerry* and *The Dukes of Hazzard*, be there, doing what they're doing, instead of here. If we didn't have to eat supper, we probably never would. Just sit back with a bag of chips and an orange soda, long as there was power on the T.V.

"Chow time!" That's Hank, our counselor. "Up and at 'em, guys!" He's O.K. Wears jeans, a sport shirt, and a V-neck sweater. Wants to be a buddy type, not a psychologist type. But it's like he's cheerleading us all the time. What a drag.

We don't sit on long benches. It's a regular room to eat in, like people have who live in real houses. We're sitting around a table and there's homemade meat loaf, and peas and mashed potatoes. Housemother cooked it. A T.V. dinner would be so great! Or a McDonald's!

"Don't you like my meat loaf? You didn't even try it, Gregory." That's Geronimo's real name, and he's not about to bother with this stuff. He's got plenty of Mars bars hidden, smuggled in from outside.

Dessert is green Jell-O with Dream Whip on top. James thinks that's wonderful—piles it on the spoon and jiggles it, watching the sparkly jewels. Then he sucks it in and out. He gets seconds and wants mine, too. I don't mind. He can have it if he likes little-kid food that much. Hank smiles his way through the meal.

84

After supper we're allowed to watch T.V., shoot pool, or play checkers. T.V.'s on, whatever we do, anyway. So Tyrone and me are having a checkers match. Melvin and Geronimo are knocking the billiard balls around. "C'mon, you sucker! Go in that pocket!"

Nobody's listening to the T.V. till this guy's saying, "The Bronx gang member is in Mercy Uptown Hospital in critical condition. It is not known what the dispute was about that caused the fifteen-year-old to shoot sixteen-year-old Jerry Washington of the Bronx Defenders. Police hope this will not signal all-out gang warfare in the troubled area. Jane DiDaddio is at the hospital now. Can you tell us anything more about the shooting, Jane?"

Melvin and Geronimo lay down their pool cues. Tyrone knocks over the checkerboard getting to the T.V. He doesn't blame me for it, even though he was winning. They're standing in front of the T.V. like they're hypnotized.

"I'm here at Mercy Hospital, Tom, where, as you know, the young gang member is fighting for his life. There have been three deaths so far this year, all young gang members." Blah, blah, blah. All she's really worrying about is if her hair looks good on the camera, and that man's suit they always wear with the big bow on the blouse.

Tyrone and Melvin are sweating. But Geronimo stays cool—except his eyes. They get darker and deeper. If you leaned toward him, you might fall in.

"What'd this guy do?! Why'd they blow him away?!"

"Yeah, what'd they do it for!?" Ernie and Tyrone are begging him to tell them.

"Don't have to be no reason. Maybe just to show they wasn't nobody to mess with. You got to do it, or you're out of the club. They kill you on the street if you don't show all the time you're not scared."

Melvin's so nervous, he just makes it to the bathroom. When he comes out, he starts picking on James till he's got him crying. Then he says, "What are you crying for, baby? Want your mama?"

Luckily Hank comes in. "O.K., fellows. Time to hit the sack! What's going on here? Melvin, lay off James! You're a big guy, and you're supposed to protect the younger kids." Yeah, yeah, sure! That'll be the day!

We're in our bunks. The dormitory's got curtains with flowers on them and yellow paint on the walls, but we're still stacked up like in a pet store. The big, important guys get to be on the bottom so they don't have to climb, and they can grab embarrassing parts of you when you're trying to get up to your bunk.

86

Now's the time they're all waiting for. Lights have been out about fifteen minutes. It'll be an hour before Hank checks out the dorm again. Geronimo reaches under the mattress, but it's not really under, 'cause the housemother's onto that. He's got it arranged so there's a place slashed *inside* the mattress cover. She hasn't found it yet, and when she does, he'll fix another hiding place. So he's pulling out these magazines and a flashlight. At first he just stretches out grinning, teasing everybody that he's not gonna let 'em look. But they're out of their bunks like monkeys coming down from the trees and snatching at a pile of bananas.

You know what these magazines are, you can see 'em on the subways. But I don't understand. I mean, I *do* sort of, I'm interested in finding out about certain things. But these magazines are *crazy*! It's in color, like television, and these people are doing *weird* stuff! Well, I saw my mother with my half brother inside, and I know the baby had to get in there somehow. I even know how, of course. But I never saw people with their faces so strange, while these weird things are kind of happening. They look like Melvin when he's stomping worms!

And all that laughing and nervous jumping around Tyrone and Ernie and the rest of 'em do. They've got it all wrong, all mixed up! They're all the time hurting and hurting everything, these guys. Well, I don't want to be like them. So I'm not fighting for a look at their dumb magazines. I just want to go to sleep like James is.

Suddenly, in his dreams, James hollers, "Mama! Mama!" and Melvin turns toward the sound. He's got a bad, ugly look on his face.

"Watch out, James!" I yell.

Melvin reaches up and pulls James by his pajama leg right out of the top bunk, down to the floor. "Here's yo' mama, you little faggot!" Melvin pushes the open magazine into James' face. Poor James— he's not even woken up yet—starts crying.

"Say it's yo' mama. Say it or I'll bust ya, faggot!"

Faggot! That's the worst thing they can call you. I don't know what it is, but it's something they're scared of, so they've got to stomp it. Tyrone jumps on James, pins him so he can't turn his head away, and Melvin keeps shoving the magazine at him. "Show which one is yo' mama! I ain't gonna let you go till you do!"

Geronimo doesn't even look up. Ernie says, "Ah, leave the kid alone," and keeps on looking at the pictures.

And me—I turn into a maniac. I'm screaming, "Leave the kid alone!" and making a flying tackle onto Tyrone's back. My arms and legs are going like windmills. They're so surprised, it takes 'em a little while to grab me off and twist my arms in back. Even then, I'm trying to spit on Melvin.

"Let the little sucker go," Geronimo tells them, and they have to. Whatever Geronimo says, they do.

"Counselor's coming!" Everybody dives for their bunks.

Must be midnight. Moonlight's spying through the flower curtains. James isn't crying anymore. He's sleeping with his arms up protecting his face. Melvin's curled like a baby with his thumb in his mouth.

I'm not sorry I did what I did. But does it mean I'm getting like them? Oh, please, please, don't let me be like them!

I'm sweating, even though it's cool in Margaret Mary's garden. If anybody around here knew about this stuff, they'd never let me *near* Dawn Marie again.

8

I go with Walter a couple of times more to the rink.
I mean, I want to and I don't. There's this feeling
when I'm rolling: All this air's going past me and
I'm flying somewhere. Maybe I'll just take off, like
"We're American Airlines," and Brooklyn'll only be
little funny lines and dots way down there.

I'm zooming in these big circles while Walter's
coaching the Club on three-turns. He's so nice, Walter. He doesn't bug me to "come and join the gang"
or anything. Then Jerry calls, "Hey, Robert, your
power strokes are getting good! Why don't you try
a Mohawk? You could do it. See, if you keep an eye
on this straight-out arm, tuck your heel in here, and
rock over, you're just naturally going to do it."

I try it for him, but then he goes back to working
the circles, first on his left foot, then on his right,
his eyes clamping him onto that line so he can't fall

off, and I'm flying around by myself again.

It's better if I don't start getting into this. What's the sense? The next place I end up, there probably isn't even going to be a rink.

> *"Ah, my lovely green isle,*
> *Once again you will smile,*
> *And the prisons no more hold our dreams!"*

The little brown wood radio on top of the broken T.V. in Margaret Mary's kitchen is rolling out Irish songs.

"A happy St. Patrick's Day!" she says to me. "I'm getting ready to go feed the dogs in the park, and Walter's gone to the candy store for his paper."

I want to get the paper for Walter, but he likes to see his retired buddies. It's their office, the candy store. They come in with grandchildren in strollers, "minding the baby for the daughter." Walter's got a little money coming from being in World War II, but he doesn't like to take it easy. He says, "The good Lord didn't give me this strong back and arms for nothing. They're to take care of Margaret Mary. And I hope to be doing that till the day I die." So he washes up those giant pots at the restaurant.

Margaret Mary takes the "Kiss Me I'm Irish" button and puts it on her sweater. She's also got a green paper shamrock she cut out. That's pinned to her hat.

"If you're finished breakfast, I'll walk along with you, Robert. That is, if you're going toward the park." I can find papers anywhere, so I push along-

91

side her with the bags of dog food in my cart.

"It's really spring again. When I was small, I couldn't believe how one day the trees were dead, and the next there were these baby buds rocking in little green cradles on the branches. And pussy willows! I thought they really were tiny cats curled in there sleeping." Then she says, "Robert, are you happy staying with Walter and me?"

So many things start jangling around in my mind. A few weeks ago people treated me like I was an animal, begging for a piece of leftover food. And I was just waiting for somebody to kick my butt, because they're always going to do it, even the "nice" ones. With Margaret Mary and Walter I'm not a dog anymore. They must be crazy to kind of like me the way they do. I guess this must be happiness.

"Yes," I mumble to Margaret Mary.

You'd think I put a gold crown on her head or something. Then she starts greeting everybody she sees. "Happy St. Patrick's Day, Mrs. Bernstein! Happy St. Patrick's Day, Miss Feldman!

"Oh, I know," she says to me, "Jewish people don't celebrate St. Patrick's Day, but that doesn't matter. We all feel the same things. I often go in the synagogue over on 13th Street, and I have a nice, peaceful time, even if I don't know what they're saying. It's the Bible language, you know. I myself came up Catholic, but I like to go to Presbyterian or Lutheran or Methodist services sometimes too. Now Walter, he'll go to Christmas Mass, but the sisters—they were stricter in the old days—smacked his hand with a ruler, and that about finished him for going to church a lot."

We're at Methodist Hospital, and Harry, the hot-dog man, is in his usual place in front. That smell of sauerkraut and boiled dogs pulls you by the nose right toward his stand. Makes you hungry even if you're not.

Margaret Mary says, "Would you like a hot dog, Robert?"

"Oh, no, thank you, breakfast was fine!"

"How's your feet, Harry, dear?" she says.

He's standing on a bunch of cardboard and he's got burlap wrapped around his shoes. "All these doctors, I'd give 'em a free hot dog every day if they'd fix *my* dogs."

"Have you tried a soak in slippery-elm bark? My grandmother swore by it for painful feet."

"I tried everything." He's got customers, so we move on.

"I think pushing that heavy wagon up to the park is what's breaking his feet," I say to Margaret Mary.

"Oh, I know. I'm sure it's just that very thing. It's so cruel. It makes me think of Our Lord and the Stations of the Cross. I wouldn't tell that to Father O'Flynn, but Seventh Avenue would be the first station, and Eighth Avenue would be the second, and so on all the way across the park to where Harry lives. But maybe we have to suffer so we know what He suffered. Do you think so, Robert?"

She's asking *me*? The way I see it, Margaret Mary, there's some who do most of the suffering, and some who do hardly any. Why this is I don't know, but I hope your God is working on it. Naturally, I don't tell Margaret Mary that. It might hurt her.

"Yeah, that must be it. Well, here's where I get off. There's a lot of *New York Times*es on this block."

"Thank you for carrying my bags, Robert." Knocks me out the way she's always saying "Thank you"!

"Oh, you're welcome." I wave at her from the corner. She waves back like she's waving a flag.

A lot of time goes by, including another Fatal Friday that didn't turn out to be so fatal. Walter went down to see Al again about that "electric bill." "Lucky stiff has went on vacation for a month," he says. Yeah, sure. A police sergeant getting a month's vacation. That'll be the day. This is one guy who really tries not to get his wife all upset, so maybe ol' Robert is going to be around awhile longer.

Dawn Marie hasn't come to Marsha's for a whole week and I know the sisters wouldn't exactly appreciate my hanging around her school. Did her mother see me walking with her that time? Or did Mrs. O'Conner—with her long nose from sniffing around corners and her long arms from leaning out the window and her telescope eyes that can spot two kids holding hands three blocks away—did Mrs. O'Connor go up to Dawn Marie's mother in the supermarket? "That boy that Margaret Mary has took in, he's been seein' your Dawn M'ree. Now, I don't want to butt in . . . " butt, butt, butt.

Or could it have been Mr. Gribowski, always

standing in front of his house, not moving, never saying anything? Just a chunk of a man, carved out of a square block of wood, with rubbers on his square feet and a hat on his square head. His heavy eyes move, though, following me down the street like I was a Russian spy trying to steal the neighborhood. Did he snap open his wooden teeth just once? "That boy is after your daughter, Mrs."

So I'm dragging my cart around through the streets in the daytime and trying to smile at Walter's little-kid jokes at night. Also, I've got to keep shoveling in Margaret Mary's two-ton productions, or she'll be worrying about my appetite.

So now it's Saturday A.M. Margaret Mary barrels down from upstairs in a panic because a couple of pairs of Walter's shorts and some undershirts need to go to the Laundromat. Would I take them? Never saw her worry about something like that, but sure, I'll take them over.

The Laundromat is on the corner of Seventh Avenue: Ye Olde English Laundromat. It's painted white inside and out, with strips of fake brown wood in V's and plastic roses tacked like they were growing on the walls. The owner thinks she's pretty elegant. She's got rings on both hands, and the dress is an A&S special from the "Mature Women's Department" (that means hefty). But she only fusses in once in a while to boss Gladys around. Gladys is the manager.

Usually I don't mind going to the Laundromat.

95

Watching the customers is kind of interesting. But not today. The thought of being pinned down, waiting for the wash cycle, the rinse, the spin, and an empty dryer—it's Boresville.

Boresville, did I say? Not now! Her soft fluff of hair is bent over a book, and she looks up now and then to see how her laundry is doing in the machine. Hey! Margaret Mary was upstairs, probably looking out the window, which she likes to do. So that's why Walter's shorts needed washing right away!

The seat next to Dawn Marie is empty, but I'm hesitating. Should I just sit down? Maybe her mother's been telling her not to talk to a crumb like me? Her eyes travel up from my sneakers to my face, and she shines her smile at me so quick and sweet, I know it's O.K.

"Hi!"

"Hi."

"Err—what are you doing here?" She's doing the laundry, stupid!

"I'm doing the laundry for my mother. She has a lot of work, so I help when I don't have school."

"I'm here for Margaret Mary."

"Oh. . . ."

"What are you reading?"

She shows me. "It's my French textbook."

"That's Paris, isn't it?" I point to the color photograph in the front. There's the Eiffel Tower; I've seen it in *National Geographic*. And a wide avenue with a big arch at the end, and real thick, green trees along it. None of your cheap, Brooklyn type of trees.

"Yes. It's a beautiful place," she says. Did you ever think of going there, to France?"

She puts her head on the side, thinking. "I would like to go someday. Your accent gets really perfect if you speak French all the time. But first I'd have to do my nurse's training and get a job. Then, for a vacation, you know, sometime I might go."

"I'd go right now, if I could. Get on that airplane, sit myself down, have the stewardess bring me one of those trays. Maybe I'd even have me a glass of pink wine, and I'd settle back and just feel that ol' ocean sliding away under me till she says, 'Paris, France'!"

"I *would* like to sit at one of those restaurants outside and watch the people. And at night there's strings of lights everywhere, and boats that go on the river with people dancing." She shows me a picture of that.

" 'Scuse me. Is that your machine? It's stopped," this old lady, the type that keeps her hat and coat on in the Laundromat, tells Dawn Marie.

"Oh, thank you! I forgot!" Dawn Marie leaps up and starts pulling the clothes out of number 11.

"Your wash'd come whiter with New Marv." The old lady pokes at Dawn Marie's wash. You can tell her hands spend most of their time when she's home in hot water and suds. "New Marv is a thousand times better."

"Yes? Well, thank you for telling me. Next time I'll get New Marv and try it."

"I've did my bedspread over here, and it came out good. Got to do that bedspread every week, 'cause of the dog. He gets up on it and pretends I don't see him. Opens one eye, shuts it quick. You'd laugh if you saw his face! I tell him, 'Bitsy, what are you doing on my bed? Mama sees you, you bad boy!' "

Dawn Marie is listening patiently and smiling at the old dame. I wish Bitsy's mama would go away and let Dawn Marie and me get back to Paris.

Oh, geez, I forgot Walter's shorts and stuff. Quickly I toss them in number 10 and slam the door. By this time Dawn Marie has loaded up her dryer, and the old lady is shoving off with her bedspread in a shopping cart that's got its wheels held on with wire and a prayer. I jump up to hold the door open for her, and she says, "Have a good day, sonny."

Dawn Marie is back in her seat, and for a while we watch all the round windows with a white suds storm going on in each. Except number 10. I forgot to put in the soap! I dump the cup in and sit down, kind of embarrassed. Gladys, the Laundromat manager—she's got tired blond hair, sort of a worn-out, nice face—switches the radio to WPIX, "Love songs, nothing but love songs."

"Ayyy, Gladys!" The dippy guy who fixes the machine starts teasing her.

Reaching out, high over the airplane takeoff noise of washers going into spin cycles, comes a teenage voice, with these guys behind him going, "Ooo-Wah, Ooooo-Wah":

> *All you have to do is touch my hand*
> *To show you understand,*
> *And something happens to me*
> *That's some kind of wonderful . . .*
> *Some kind of sweetness,*
> *Some kind of warmth,*
> *Some kind of softness,*
> *Wonderful, wonderful . . . wonderful*

You know this guy's good-looking, with slick, black hair, and he's smiling and holding the mike like he was kissing it. I really feel this music all the way through me. Mr. Cool hits it one more time, and I don't dare look at Dawn Marie—it's *me* singing. This song is for us.

"Oh, that's one of my favorites!" Dawn Marie says. "It's The Drifters!" Seeing that I don't know who or what is "The Drifters," she explains. "It's a fifties song. I have a collection of fifties records. You can borrow it if you want." Margaret Mary and Walter have a 78 record player that handles jokers like Caruso and Tchaikovsky doing "The Dance of the Sugar-Plum Fairy." So I thank her, tell her sometime I will.

Suddenly she jumps up. "My dryer is stopped."

Walter's shorts are ready for the dryer, so I toss them in and start helping her with folding. She shakes everything, then smooths it and wraps it over real neat. Some sheets and things are big. We have to each hold out our corners and bring them together, then I meet her in the middle for the final fold, which is so close it's embarrassing.

This little kid is leaning against the benches, one foot curled on top of the other. He's looking through the hole of a big doughnut at us, pretending it's a camera, I guess.

"Hi," Dawn Marie says. The kid is shy, so he starts bumping his doughnut along the tops of the washers like it was a car.

"Brian! Don't do that! Be good and sit down." This is a situation where the mother is always telling the kid to sit down, and he's Luke Skywalker or a race-car driver, and he can't sit down.

Dawn Marie picks up one of the Laundromat price lists and creases it this way and that way. When she's finished, it's an alligator with jaws that can bite. Brian sits in his seat, cruising it up in the air and over the bench, going, *"Arrrrr!!"*

The mother shakes her head. "He drives me crazy!" But she's smiling at Dawn Marie.

That's it. Everybody smiles at Dawn Marie. She's beautiful, but that's not the real reason. There's something about her. She's in the same world as me and everybody else—am I glad about that! But she doesn't think people are a pain in the neck or ugly. So, suddenly, they're not.

She's got all her stuff in her shopping cart, and I put my little bundle on top and take the handle. "Oh, you don't have to do that."

100

"It's O.K. I like to push these things. We have here a Plymouth-type shopping cart, I'd say. And that one over there is more of a Caddy. Observe the gorgeous red paint job and four rubber-tire wheels instead of only two so you don't have to bend your back dragging it. It's high class. When I get rich, I'm going to buy you a Mercedes shopping cart." She grins. I grin. Say, I'm a real comedian when I'm with her!

Then she turns very serious. "Do you think you're going to be rich? I don't mean because of the Mercedes shopping cart!" She's pinking up again. "But there's this boy I know, he's a friend of the family. His father went to high school with my father, and he's going to be a lawyer just so he can get a lot of money. He says he's going to buy a certain kind of car, a Porsche, that costs thirty-five thousand dollars! I don't think you should be like that! I mean, sometimes lawyers are good. They can help you if someone is trying to do an injustice, like taking away your house. But you shouldn't want to be one just for the money."

"Yeah. Well, the thing I *really* want to be, I doubt I'd get rich. I'd be happy just to get in the chorus line. They give you maybe about a hundred bucks a week, which would be fine by me. Of course, if you're a star in the show, you might get five hundred, or even a thousand dollars a week. It's the roller-skating show I'm talking about."

Hey, this is crazy! I tell Walter I'm not interested; I don't want to train. Now I'm telling Dawn Marie this is what I really want to be! I guess I haven't got that flying feeling out of my system. And Walter kind of wanting me to be his roller-skating "son."

"It would be a lot of hard work, training and training, but Walter said he thinks I could do it. He said I had a nice line, that I hold myself straight, you know." Now I'm blushing. She'll think I'm a liar, for sure.

"When I'm a nurse, I'll come in my uniform and see you every night in the roller-skating show."

"O.K. It's a date."

Dawn Marie looks down at the ground. "I heard from Mrs. Polini your mother's dead. I'm really sorry, Robert."

"Oh, well, I'm used to it now."

"She must have been nice if she was your mother."

"Yeah, uh, well . . ."

"You don't have to talk about it if you mind. . . ."

"Hey, it's O.K.! It doesn't bother me at all."

But I *do* mind! I don't want to talk about my mother to anybody—except maybe Dawn Marie. It all comes busting out.

"She was sixteen and she wasn't married when she got me." (Oh, geez, I shouldn't tell Dawn Marie that! She's Catholic and they don't allow girls to have kids unless they're married. But I can't stop.) "Like they say, everybody's got to do their own thing, and hers wasn't wiping little kids' noses, that's all.

"So sometimes she took care of me for a while, and then she'd get a new boyfriend. And there I'd be, over in the corner, lookin' at 'em, and the guy says, 'Oh God, that kid is always watching me. Here, take your truck, go play outside. And quit the cryin'!'

"After a while, I learned. *Don't cry.* They can't stand you if you cry. *Don't laugh*, either. *Don't nothin'!* After a while I just watched, out of the way. My eyes must've got big from watching, and my mouth, it was like filled up with concrete."

Shut up! You're saying too much! She'll think you're weird or disgusting! But her eyes are looking right in mine. And I can't stop talking anyway.

"So some neighbors called the police 'cause she used to leave me locked in the room and go to the movies. And that's when they started putting me in foster homes."

She's trembling a little. "Did your mother die when you were in a foster home?"

"Well, as a matter of fact, she's not exactly dead. I just told Margaret Mary and Walter that so they wouldn't send me back."

"Oh. Well, where is she now?"

"I don't know. She's always moving around, new apartment, new guy. She doesn't need me. She's always got a guy to take care of her. Believe me, she wouldn't want to know where I am. She might have to take me back."

"Were the foster-home people nice to you?"

"Some were, some weren't. Mostly it's just a business, you know, keeping kids, getting paid for the room and board. That's why I can't believe it's for

real that Margaret Mary and Walter are doing this.
I hope I can stay, but you never know. They might
get to thinking I'm a drag."

"Oh, no! They wouldn't! They're really happy
you came!"

"Yeah, but there's this other thing. I feel, sometimes, I feel like I could get really crazy mad, go
vicious, you know, maybe wind up hurting somebody. I'm scared I might be getting like—like this
guy Joe. He used to beat up this woman I know.
And Margaret Mary and Walter would sure get rid
of me then!"

"I don't think you'd *ever* hurt another person,
Robert. And you're happy here. I mean with Margaret Mary and Walter, so you wouldn't want to
do . . . what you just said."

We've been leaning on a wall around somebody's
little brownstone garden. There's pansies with those
little growly faces, and those bushes that shoot off
yellow fireworks. I'm beat, like I walked about a
thousand miles to get here.

"I didn't have anything like you had when I was
growing up." Dawn Marie starts talking, and her
voice is softer and quieter than ever. "Like I told
you, my mother and father are very strict. I'm their
only child, you know, and they worry something
might happen to me. I go to the same school they
did, but they don't understand. Even St. Saviour's
has changed. I mean, nowadays the kids are different. In my class the girls think I'm sort of babyish
compared to them. I don't care. I mean, I don't

104

really want to wear lots of makeup and hang out. So my friends tease and say I'm weird, that I like French more than I like boys. Nadine's my best friend. She's from India, and her folks don't want her to go with boys either. It isn't that we don't like boys. But you can't always be making your parents upset, can you? And we really *like* studying and going to school. So I guess that makes me weird."

"Oh, no! I think it's great that you read all those books and everything. I think you're fine, just fine the way you are. I wouldn't change one fingernail of you, for anything!"

We're at her steps. She wants to take the cart now, but I won't let her. I lift it with one hand, run up the steps, and park it at the door. I wouldn't care if her mother, her father, *and* her uncle from Jersey were watching!

She goes in and I take the steps at one jump. It's like I just coughed up a big chunk of concrete.

9

I'm picking up bagels for Margaret Mary and Walter's Sunday-morning breakfast. Personally, I prefer to stick to the Danishes or Munchkins from Dunkin' Donuts. A bagel's kind of like an iron doughnut to me.

But Margaret Mary says, "My mother used to take me and my sister next door to visit Mrs. Greenberg. And they'd have coffee and bagels when it was Mrs. Greenberg's turn, and scones when it was my mother's turn to have Mrs. Greenberg. And we'd love the bagels because we didn't get a chance to have them very often. You'd have to go way over to another neighborhood to get them in those days.

"I don't know to this day if bagels are that wonderful, or if it's the memories that make them taste so good—my mother taking time to sit down for a little while and have a chat with Mrs. Greenberg,

106

and me under the table trying to get Mrs. Greenberg's cat, Mitzi, to eat some bagel, and Mitzi looking at me like I was crazy."

So it's bagels and cream cheese for Margaret Mary and Walter, and a special kind of almond Danish from way up Fifth Avenue that Margaret Mary gets for me.

Now, it just so happens I'm going by across the street from St. Saviour's, the church part, and Mass is getting out. There's a bunch of these ladies in front. They look like pigeons, pecking and poking at the latest gossip.

One of them's sure to be saying, "Well, I never saw nobody so drunk as May's husband last night. She had to drag him down the hall into the apartment, poor soul!"

"Oh, my, yes! They were gettin' ready to give me the last rites, I was so bad after my operation!"

"Bee-yoo-tee-ful funeral he had."

There's one, her hair is stiffer and blacker than anybody's hair could be. It's holding up the most important hat in the crowd; this hat looks like a giant coffee cake. She's *got* to be saying, "This neighborhood is just deterioratin' with all the low types comin' in. My husband says we ought to think of goin' out to Jersey." She looks across the street and starts nailing me with these too-close-together eyes. I don't know why, till her husband separates out from the men standing around under their Sunday hats. He takes her arm, and Dawn Marie, in a little hat made out of flowers, is running toward them!

107

That's Dawn Marie's mother and father! The mother nudges the father, and I get the freez-o stare from both of them. They practically yank her away down the street, but she sneaks a look at me when they have to stop to gab with the reverend who runs their church.

Back at the house the almond Danish is sitting in front of me. All I see is Dawn Marie's face, and her eyes saying, "Robert, I'm a prisoner here with them! You know if I could, I'd come be with you this beautiful Sunday morning."

Well, maybe I'm getting carried away, her eyes saying all that and everything. But it was only for *me*, whatever they said.

Next day I just happen to be on Eighth Avenue and 6th, pushing a big load of newspapers. I look up from the ground, where my eyes usually are, and I see there's a long, yellow bus parked in front of Dawn Marie's high school. Kids are holding a bed sheet out the windows that says, "Dunk Queen of Angels!"

They must be going to a game. The sisters are flapping around trying to get this bunch of green-plaid-skirt girls on board. Also, there's a coach with a whistle around his neck and St. Francis Xavier on the back of his jacket. That must be the boys' part of St. Saviour's. The coach is trying to get his boys rounded up and onto the bus. Never seen so many guys with haircuts! But they've got to get the girls on first, sitting down one side of the bus, with the sister riding backward in the front seat, and then the boys, with the aisle between them. Well, you can imagine how easy that is! Like putting socks on an octopus, my day-care teacher would say when she was trying to get us all dressed to go outside.

I'm enjoying the show. This guy thinks he's real cool, making remarks to the girls. He's got straight, navy-blue high-water pants and a straight little tie going down the front of his shirt, and the same straight, "good boy" haircut they all have. A buddy shoves him right into the mess of girls; and of course they start screaming and laughing. "Sister! Help!" All of them except . . . Dawn Marie. She's not being proud or trying to be different. But there's a quiet place where she is. You'd see her if there were a thousand people milling around. I'm trying to make a getaway, but she sees me. Oh, why did I have to be coming down Eighth Avenue just now?

I want her to wave "Hi," but I know she can't. Her girl friends would tease her, and Sister would be shocked. A nice girl wouldn't wave at a trash picker. How do I know she even wants to? Her face is asking me, "Please understand, Robert!" but why should I? If she can let that musclehead with his basketball letter and "cute" yellow-and-blue jacket stand right by her and practically drool on her, why can't she say "Hi" to me?

Well, hell, I don't need her to say "Hi" to me. I got along fine without knowing her for fourteen years. I can still get along fine. I'm not even giving her the satisfaction of looking back when the bus comes chasing me up to 9th and passes me, burping

109

black smoke in my face. Kid leaning out the window beans me with an apple core.

For three days I'm walking around talking to myself like an old wino. "When I see her, I'm giving her the brush. This is one dude who is *not* off his rocker over her. I got plenty else to think about— planning stuff I might do after I bust out of here."

Then I see her over on Seventh Avenue with her Indian girl friend. "Hi, Robert!" She's smiling and waving.

"Oh, hi, Dawn Marie!!"

I stand watching them go on up the avenue, and I'm the happiest guy in Brooklyn, Queens, *and* Manhattan. You could throw in Staten Island and the Bronx, too.

So that's the way the days go, into April. It's crazy luck for a bozo like me to be staying with nice folks like Margaret Mary and Walter. Of course, we just had another phony Friday. Margaret Mary's getting dizzy spells this time, and Walter's telling us, "You're not gonna believe this. Al broke his leg on vacation!" I'm betting on Al to run away with Elizabeth Taylor next Friday *if* his leg gets better.

I appreciate what they're all the time doing for me, and I work real hard, trying not to be a drag on them. But don't get me wrong. No offense to Margaret Mary and Walter, it's a little bit boring here compared to just seeing Dawn Marie go down the block.

And you know how it is—when you want to see something, you're looking so hard that *Wham! Shazaam!* it's there! I mean, not really, but for a week I got her poppin' up all over Park Slope. She's coming out of the cleaners' on Fifth Avenue and 10th. She's a block ahead of me, shopping on Seventh Avenue. Then she's dancing into the park and the big lions smile down on her like they wouldn't for anybody else. Soon as I hurry up, of course, she's gone.

But what do you know! This time it's really her walking down Prospect Park West. Only it's not like regular people's walking. The way she walks, she's straight, but maybe there's a little breeze where she goes and it's kind of swaying her.

The bench people don't see anything but a streak with sneakers for the two blocks till I catch up with her. I give her my Paul Newman smile and say, "Going someplace?" Why do I always do this? She's not going *no* place, stupid.

"I'm going over to the library for some social studies research Sister gave us." She looks like maybe she's even glad it's me.

"Hey, this must be some kind of coincidence! I was just thinking of going over there and checking out the place myself!" Liar! She's gonna know you don't go to libraries. A bonehead like you.

"Oh, you haven't seen this library? You'll like it. I mean, it's so big, and it has these sort of flat gold statues on the sides of the doors. I always stop and look at them. And, of course, the books. They must have a million books. Any book you ever wanted, they'd have it."

"Sure," I say. "Sure, I'd like to see all those books."

We're coming into the plaza. This mob of cars is charging around in a circle, shooting out of Flatbush Avenue and peeling off down Eastern Parkway or up Prospect Park West. And looking down at everything, there it is—not the tallest, but what's got to be the heaviest building in Brooklyn, the public library.

Dawn Marie and me start toward it, and I mean it's a hike, the plaza's so wide. Going up the steps, she says, "I always feel like it's Egypt when I get here. I mean, a person is so small; and the buildings are so big. You know, like the pyramids."

I nod. There's a shish-kebab-and-falafel joint on Seventh Avenue, with these Egyptian pictures painted on the walls. "I know what you mean."

The glass doors are maybe four stories high, and we're standing looking up at the gold statues she was talking about. Well, they're not exactly statues. More like a stone story of some kind, with kings and some lions and eagles that are kings, too. And there're professors reading books and measuring and weighing stuff. All of them are bare chested, which is a little embarrassing considering some of these flat, gold types are ladies. But they're so important, looking somewhere out there. You know they'd never be embarrassed.

I'm first through the heavy glass turning doors,

112

figuring I'll push them out of the way for her. Then I see this dude waiting for this lady to go in front of him and *then* pushing. Oh, geez, wrong again.

Going up the escalator, I make *sure* she's ahead of me. I can't help noticing—though you can bet I don't bend over and sniff—that there's a soft, light-pink smell coming off her, some kind of soap, maybe. I wish this escalator would just keep on going, with everybody else getting off except us. She steps away so neat at the top, and I'm stumbling off after her when the steps flatten under me.

"The young adult room is downstairs. I was going to return this book. . . ." She holds it out for me to see. "If you'd like to look at it, I don't have to return it yet." There's a dark, scribbled drawing on the cover, which turns out to be this guy and a horse, fighting something, or just riding like crazy. I flip over the pages—words all gray down every page. Looks serious.

"I took it out because of my name. You see, it's *Dawn Wind*!"

Yeah, now I notice it is *Dawn*. "Hey, what do you know? It's got your name!"

"It's just a coincidence." She starts blushing like I might think she was really in a book. "At first it seemed harder than the other books, but then it was so good! It was sad for a while, because this boy—it's in England, and it's historical—this boy is captured and taken away from his people and has to be very brave, and he can't get back home for years. And there's this girl—at the beginning she's

113

very young, younger than he is, and he takes care of her. But at the end, they're sort of the same age that they could be together. I mean, not the *same* age!" She's all flustered. "When they're young, they wouldn't be boy and girl friends, of course. But when he's older, then she's older, too, and they know they're going to be together always, till they both die."

We're sitting at a table, and people are looking up from their magazines and notebooks, squeezing their eyebrows at us. She puts her hand on her mouth like it's a crime for us to be talking in the library, but our eyes are laughing. She jumps up, whispering that she's got to get her research books and she'll be right back. Pretty soon she is, with a load of stuff to work on.

For a long time, we're there. She's turning over the pages and writing in her notebooks, pressing her lips together sometimes, like a business type, which is pretty funny. I'm supposed to be reading *Dawn Wind*, but I'm sneaking looks at Dawn Marie. I mostly flip the pages, but I stop at this one picture. It's a boy, maybe fourteen, what you'd call good-looking. He could take care of things, even big trouble, like the war that is going on in back of him.

"Robert, I never noticed before, but he looks a lot like you!"

"Nah!" I whisper back. "Nah! This guy's good-lookin'." And I think, *he* knows where he's going, not always getting pushed around.

"Please check out your books in fifteen minutes! The library is closing at seven" comes out of the loudspeaker.

"I didn't know we'd been here so long!" Dawn Marie looks scared. "I should have been home an hour ago!" She grabs up her little red pocketbook and her homework, and she's running down the marble floor to the exit. I'm tailing her, worried because she looks like that. What's her mother gonna do to her, anyway? Beat her?

I catch up on the escalator.

"I really knew it was getting late," she says. Her head's down. "It's just that my mother never wants me to be out when it's getting dark, especially by the park and *especially* with a boy. But I don't really think I'm doing anything wrong! And I don't think that every boy wants to do something dirty to me!"

"Are they gonna punish you?" I ask after a moment.

"Well, my mother will be mad. She'll say, 'You know you're not supposed to be by the park at night. A man could put his hands on you!' And my father won't speak to me. That's worse than punishment. He'll just look like I was doing something bad to our family and to God and everything. When my grandmother was alive, she'd say, 'Don't pull in so tight on a little horse's reins!' She got me the blue shoes, you know, with real heels, when my mother said I was too young."

"Oh, geez, Dawn Marie, it's my fault. Couldn't

you tell 'em that?" But I knew she'd get in worse trouble if she told them I was with her.

"Please, let's not talk about it," she says.

The glass doors twirl us outside and Brooklyn's going purple. The pine trees in the park are black, with a gold splash where the sun is. Above, it's serious blue with outer-space light in back of that.

She's standing on the front steps looking around like a little kid getting a present. Maybe she's forgetting she's in bad trouble.

"What if space people are up there waiting to land, Dawn Marie! It would be right here, in front of the library, because they'd see it from a thousand miles up and know this great big circle was where they're supposed to park the spaceship."

"Oh, yeah! Any minute we might see them land!" We watch for a little while more, sort of waiting. Then she says, "Robert, I better go."

All along Seventh Avenue she's trying to talk as if everything's O.K. But our time is spoiled. Why do they always have to do that? People don't care about their own kids. They're all the time just figuring what'll make *them* look good.

"You mustn't think my folks are mean. They're not." There's ESP between Dawn Marie and me. "It's just . . . they don't understand. They think it's still like when they were teenagers and their parents were strict with them." I nod my head, but I wish I could punch 'em out.

Business people are hurrying out of the subway

116

from the city, picking up a pizza or a frozen dinner. They can't wait to take off their heels and jackets and drop in front of the T.V. We can see in the windows. The neighborhood is sitting at their kitchen tables, kids reaching for the Wonder Bread or the soda; the mom's standing up passing stuff off the stove. The father's sitting there in his chair, but he's still driving his truck through bad traffic.

On the corner of 9th and Fifth Avenue, there's a lady trying to give her newspaper away. *Awake*, something religious. She's standing there with flowers all over her dress; black, laced-up shoes with places for the bunions; hat going straight ahead. Could be anybody's aunt. Awake for what? I want to say, "Lady, it's better if you stay sleeping. Then you won't know how bad the scene is out here."

Dawn Marie hands her back the paper. "Oh, no, I'm sorry. I'm Catholic. But thank you anyway." And she smiles so maybe the lady won't feel so discouraged.

Near her corner I get the message. Dawn Marie won't say it; she's too nice. But it wouldn't be smart for me to show up like I was bringing her home from a date. There'd be her mother, glaring between the curtains. "Who is that nothing she's with?!"

"A nobody! Who does he think he is, walking down the street with *my* daughter?" her father's growling, biting on his cigar.

"Well, uh, I better go, Dawn Marie. I feel awful that you might get in trouble. . . ."

"Oh," she says, "it'll be all right, really. Anyway, it was pretty seeing the plaza getting dark. Thank you!" And she's gone.

She's thanking me? Here I had this great and beautiful time with her, and she's thanking me?

10

TO THE BEST MOM
FOR MY DEAR MOTHER ON MOTHER'S DAY
HAVE A HAPPY MOTHER'S DAY!

I flip open a pink fake-velvet number and read what's inside:

> She's always there,
> The One who cares,
> My Friend in need,
> A Pal indeed—
> Only you, Mom!

Yeah, sure. And I'm Paul Newman. Hey! It's O.K.! Doesn't bother me. It's just to sell stuff anyway: bunches of flowers, cards, those big boxes of candy where you've got to have a map to know which one you want.

I'm at the drugstore picking up kidney pills for Walter's back, which aches from lifting pots sometimes. The place is overdosing on roses. Most of the cards have them, and there's plastic ones stuck on perfume, nail-polish sets, you name it.

It's just to make money. If they could, they'd have Plumber's Day. "Send a lovely bouquet, in a reusable planter, to your plumber, with a card that says, 'You're always there, the one who cares. . . .' " Ha, ha! Yeah, well, like I say, I couldn't care less.

I'm looking at these pictures on the cards. They've got old-fashioned ones where the lady's wearing a long, blue hood and she's holding a baby and they both got gold circles going around their heads. Also, for the modern types, they have a mother with a tennis racquet. None of them looks like Margaret Mary. Hell, she'd make a better one than any of them!

Margaret Mary sure loves cards. Here's one I *know* she'd be crazy about. It's got this man in a white bathrobe and a beard, walking in a garden. He's holding out his hand toward a whole lot of ladies with babies up in the air. It's this kind of real photograph that's deep; you actually look inside the picture. Wonder how they do the ladies in the clouds. The poem, it's just one line: "The Love That Ne'er Ends."

Suddenly I'm up front, slapping down my money. I tell myself, "She's always taking care of Walter and Heather-Belle and Big Boy and even me. She's like a mother to half the neighborhood, and that's

120

taking in everything up to Prospect Park."

Buying this card is making me very happy, even though it's three bucks, envelope included. It's big as a magazine and that kind of picture has *got* to be expensive.

Should I send it? Or maybe just hand it to her? Sending it would take too long! I'm busting the pavement getting home, I want to give it to her so bad. Outside the house I put on the brakes to write, "Happy Mother's Day, from a friend," on the bottom.

But when I'm in the kitchen handing her the pills, I lose my nerve. "Are you stupid! What are you doing? Maybe it'll just remind her she didn't have any kids, make her feel bad!"

By now it's too late to get rid of this giant envelope, so I shove it at her and wait, feeling miserable.

"Why just look at this, Big Boy! I never saw such a beautiful picture! You look right in there and it's just like it's real. See that?" She's holding it in front of Big Boy's nose. And then she's trying to get Heather-Belle to look. "It's just *beautiful*," she keeps saying, and she has to wipe her reading glasses, which are steaming up. So I guess she really does like it.

"If you wiggle it back and forth like this," I show her, "it looks like the guy's moving, and the roses look like you could touch 'em."

"Wait till Walter comes home and sees this! Why, I'm sure he's never seen such a beautiful type of

121

card. And the words! I've always felt that was true about my mother, about any mother, I guess. 'The Love That Ne'er Ends'!"

"Well, would you look at that!" Walter says when he comes in the door and she holds it in his face. "It's that three-D look like you could reach in there and touch it. Would you look at that! Say! This calls for a celebration! We'll just go on over and try some of that Chicken McNugget at McDonald's. Would you like that, Margaret Mary?" She's so pleased, she doesn't know what she's doing, what with holding on to the card and trying to get ready to go to McDonald's.

So that's how we come to be dipping McNuggets into the McKetchup sauce and grinning at each other, "pleased as punch," like Margaret Mary says. And Walter and me are toasting Margaret Mary with our root beers: "For she's a jolly good fellow! She's a jolly good fellow!" Say, we could be in one of those McDonald's commercials on T.V.

After lunch I'm covering my route like *The Dukes of Hazzard*. Maybe Dawn Marie will be over at Marsha's when I get back. She's minding Marsha a lot these days. When I'm weighing my papers at Mr. Pomerantz's, he's still somewhere inside himself where it's never spring. Mr. Pomerantz, you've been living too long in Brooklyn. Me and Dawn Marie, we're going to get out of here. We're going someplace where they talk different and feel different and do things different. We're going to Paris, France!

She can practice French and study the history there. I'll . . .What will I do besides looking at her? Never gave that any thought. You're supposed to *be* something, ya dope! Doctor, lawyer, Indian chief. So I'll be an Indian chief.

My cart's doing fifty on the way back, nearly runs over three cats and two old ladies going shopping. They all turn and give me the same disgusted "Boys, they're *awful!*" look. I'm through that gate so fast, it's too surprised to moan. Parking by the porch steps, I hear Marsha.

"Robert! Robert! Oh, Robert!" Her eye is pressed against a little hole in the fence. The way the fence is rattling and bending, it sounds like she's trying to climb right through the hole.

"Marsha, wait! You'll hurt yourself! Don't worry. Robert'll come to see you. Just wait." That's Dawn Marie's voice. It's so different from other girls'! It goes along low and soft and sort of shining. If I never saw her, just heard her through a wall, I'd say she had on a long velvet dress, with big sleeves, and her hair was all ripply around her. She's the princess in the fairy tale who saved her seven brothers by being so beautiful and good. The Catholic-school uniform would be just a disguise.

"Robert, Marsha wants you to come over," she's calling through the hole.

I jump over, fly over, the gate, and slow down just in time to stroll into the Polinis' yard.

"Hey, Marsha, how ya doin'?" I say, but I'm looking at Dawn Marie. After we get Marsha quieted down, we settle into our seats on the top step. Marsha's always in the middle because that way she can have both of us next to her.

"Who's that talking to Mrs. Polini?" I can hear a lady chatting to Marsha's mom through the living room window.

"Oh, that's my mother. She's getting Mrs. Polini to sew a dress for me."

"Oh." I've never actually *met* Dawn Marie's mother, but from what she says about her and that Sunday I saw her in front of St. Saviour's, I hope I never do! "Hey! Maybe I ought to take off? I wouldn't be exactly popular with your mother."

"No, it's all right."

"You're sure?"

"*Please* stay."

"O.K. If you say so." I sit down again. Maybe I've been around awhile and her mother's changed her mind I'm some kind of criminal.

Well, what are we going to talk about? We never know, Dawn Marie and me. Doesn't matter; whatever we talk about is going to be good.

Dawn Marie seems kind of quiet. "How'd you do on your French test?"

"Oh, I got a terrible mark. Sister said I could do much better."

"I bet it wasn't terrible. What did you get?"

"Eighty-nine." She sighs.

"Hey, that's good! If I got eighty-nine on anything, I'd think I was pretty terrific."

"Well, you see, I need to do better because of the scholarship. I'm trying to get one. My folks can't afford for me to go to nursing school unless I win a scholarship."

"Well, what if you didn't go to nursing school? That wouldn't mean your life was over, would it?"

"No, but that's what I've always wanted to be. I used to watch the nurses coming out of Methodist Hospital. There's something about them; they look so calm, and sort of dignified in those white uniforms. But I would want to be in pediatrics. That's working with babies and children, you know. When I had my tonsils out, I loved how the nurses talked to the children, and even if they had to hurt them, give them shots or things like that, they would hold them and hug them."

"You'd make a beautiful nurse," I tell her.

She's embarrassed, so she takes Marsha's telephone. "Marsha, did you and your mother go shopping at A&S?"

Marsha grabs the phone for her turn. "We went on the bus. I put the token in, and the man said, 'Have a good day!' "

"Then what did you see?"

"Oh, oh, I saw Mickey Mouse!"

"Where was he?"

"In the phone store!"

"They saw this real Mickey Mouse phone in the window of the phone store on Fulton Street. If it wasn't so expensive, I'd get it for her for her birth-

125

day. But it's a hundred and twenty dollars!" Dawn Marie whispers this so Marsha won't get the wrong idea.

The voice from the living room is getting louder. "Now, Mrs. Polini, this dress has got to be ready for June fifth, that's St. Saviour's June Frolic dance. And I know you'll make it gorgeous. Dawn M'ree is goin' with the son of a friend of the family. He'll be goin' to law school when he graduates college. He's such a good-lookin' young man, Douglas! His father's Chief Clerk of the Court, you know."

Mrs. Polini is trying to say something to her, and then both their heads pop out the window and go right back in.

"Is that boy the one Margaret Mary picked up?" Mrs. Polini is going, "Shhh, Shhh!" but it doesn't do any good. Dawn Marie's mother goes on, getting louder. "I don't want him to have nothin' to do with Dawn M'ree! Who knows where he comes from? A stray dog, that's all what he is! And stray dogs can be vicious!"

Dawn Marie's crying. Marsha doesn't know what's going on, and I get up from the steps and start feeling my way home. Feeling, because I just got shot between the eyes, and I can't see so good.

Dawn Marie starts after me, but her mother shrieks out the window, "Dawn M'ree, you come right back here!"

Marsha's trying to hurry her big policeman's feet after me, too. I hear them dragging on the path behind me. "You don't go, Robert! You don't cry!"

"I'm O.K., Marsha. You better go home. I think Margaret Mary's calling me."

Margaret Mary's not home. Neither is Walter. Heather-Belle sees me, whimpers, and dives under the porch. There's a six-pack of Budweiser in the fridge. "Here's to not rememberin' nothin'." I swallow every nasty-tasting can. By the time I make it out to the porch, I'm bombed out of my skull.

Shoulda remembered, I shoulda remembered. Dawn Marie, you made me forget. I'm the stray from nowhere, and that's where I'm goin'. Me and Paul Newman hangin' out, havin' some good times together? That is a *big* laugh! Ol' Paul wouldn't be hangin' out with any vicious stray dog.

Crazy ol' gate, won't lemme out. Got to get out. Might throw up. Nail lets go—dumps me right out inna street. I don't wanna remember, but I do. Oh, Dawn Marie, I was gonna take you to Paris, France!

11

"Robert! Robert!" Margaret Mary is calling from the corner. I just keep going.

Aw, Dawn Marie, I'd take you to any dances you wanna go to. I can't dance, but thass awright. I'd let you dance with other guys and I wouldn't even be jealous, because you'd be lookin' over their shoulders at *me* while you're dancin'. They'd bring you back when the song was over. "Here's your lovely girl." You and me, we belong together.

What am I going to do? What am I going to do? I'm lost in Brooklyn again—all these damn brown houses on all these damn gray streets. Nuke Brooklyn, that's what they oughta do. Oh, geez, where am I? Must be Seventh Avenue, because there's the deli. The subway . . . The F train; I was gonna take Dawn Marie to the city! Forget it! Forget *you*, Robert. Keep going, keep going. You got to kill time, 'cause if there wasn't any time, you couldn't remember anything, right?

Cruisin' down the avenue. *Which* avenue? Here's this dumb gate again. "Lissen, you don't wanna let anybody in. You don't wanna let anybody out. You're a cranky pain-in-a-neck gate, and you better watch out. They'll get rid of you."

It's dark in the garden, but I can see all the little grinning faces. "What are you laughin' at?!" I pick up an elf off a mushroom. "Say good-bye, sucker!" *Whamm!* That elf's coming off the fence in a million pieces. *Whooeee!* That's for ear-twisting old Auntie Alice. Oh, baby boy! This one's for Dawn Marie's mother! Bucktooth rabbit gets it. This one's for my mother's five, six, I don' know, boyfriends! Squirrels, deer, Miss Muffet, they're flying in the night and crashing. I'm cursing like a Vietnam vet, and it feels *so* good. A car light shines over the wall, passing across the Virgin Mary's face. "Don't worry, Virgin Mary! I wouldn't hurt you, 'cause you love your kid and take care of him!"

"Robert! Is that you?" Margaret Mary's standing in the yellow doorway, blinking out into the dark garden. Walter shows up big behind her.

"Yeah, it's me, crazy, nice ol' lady!"

"Oh, Robert!" She's running down the path.

"Mrs. Margaret Mary, you don't even know when people are shaftin' you, and laughin' at you. But I know when they're doin' it to me, and I smash 'em!"

She's reaching toward me. "Mrs. Polini told me.

129

She told me what Dawn Marie's mother said."

I push past her, taking a kick at that lousy ol' gate. And I'm running up 16th Street.

Geez, I busted up all of Margaret Mary's little animals. Shouldna done that. But I'm gonna buy her a whole bunch of new ones, any kind she wants.

The park is spinning by on my left. All those trees, they're running and running. I stop, they stop. I must be drunk. Little Robert is drunk. No, sir, it's boyfriend number six or eight—I dunno which—*he's* drunk. Throws my toys—my fire engine with no wheels, and my jack-in-the-box that won't go back in—at the wall. I'm sniffling under the bed. She's screaming at him, "Get outa here, you crumb!"

The Park Circle—cars whirlin' around. You go halfway around and jump off. Just like the carousel. I hear it. Music's going around and around and up and down. The camel's the one I want to ride on. Those humps keep you safe. "If you start sniffling and begging, you don't go. That's *it*. I told you I can't stand it when you snivel. You don't get no ride!"

Follow the music. Big hunk of building, blockin' up the sky. Whaddya know. It's Walter's Roller Paradise! Look in the window at all those happy suckers twirling around, holding hands, smiling and gabbing to their friends and girlfriends and boyfriends. "I was gonna show you how to do your edges, Dawn Marie. Maybe Walter could evena trained us. We coulda been figure-skating partners, my arm around you, and your hand resting on mine. But not anymore. Oh, damn!"

I pick up a big piece of broken concrete, and it's going slow motion into the window. "Carousel's busted, everybody!! You don't get no more rides!" I can't think so good; the beer is hurting bad in my head. Cop cars are screaming around the circle from the 72 Precinct.

The park takes me in. "Run, brother, run." The trees pass me on, one to the other. Now I'm swimming in a giant black swimming pool. The lights over there are Dawn Marie's house and Margaret Mary's and Walter's. Can I ever get to them? I'm drowning in the black water.

How long I've been lying on the ground in the park I don't know. Getting onto my knees, then on my feet, hurts so, I can hear myself groaning. Then I'm throwing up. That beer is poison. Well, you've fixed it good for yourself. Margaret Mary and Walter would never want a son like you. Scuffling along, head down. I don't care if muggers or werewolves get me now.

Coming out of the west corner of the park, I can't help steering toward the old neighborhood for a last look. My head is murdering me! When I hit Sixth Avenue there's a squad car outside Margaret Mary's gate. They called the police on me! Did you think they wouldn't, sucker? I'm going to beat it when there's two policemen coming down *Mrs. Polini's* steps. What's going on?

131

"Robert, have you seen Marsha?" Tony, the candy-store man, is pulling on my sleeve.

"Well, I saw her in the afternoon, around two o'clock, maybe."

"No, no! After that."

"What's happened, Tony?"

"Oh, my God, she's lost, or killed, or something! Everybody's out looking for her. Her mother is prostrated, with the doctor and everything."

In all the streets people are calling, "Marsha!" They're turning over garbage cans, putting their flashlights in empty buildings. At Margaret Mary's house the lights are out. They're looking, too. The corner of 15th Street, under the streetlight, Dawn Marie's coming, her hair dark as smoke in the rays, her eyes black with worry. She sees me.

"Oh, Robert! Marsha's lost! Would you . . . ?"

"Dawn M'ree!" Her mother sounds like a fire siren from the corner. "I don't want you goin' around alone! It's dangeruss!" I guess she can't see me away from the streetlight. Dawn Marie busts out crying and runs to head her off. Me, I'm nowhere. . . .

What do I do now? Look for Marsha too? One part of me says, Buddy, you've got to take care of Number One. Nobody ever cared a damn what happened to you. Why get in a sweat over somebody else? Besides, you don't belong here anymore, getting drunk and smashing up the place like Frankenstein. They probably don't want any help from a crazy like you turned out to be. And Dawn Marie, now she knows what you're really like. Just split. You're an outlaw for real.

The other part of me sees Marsha holding out her piece of baloney. "You could have it, Robert." And hollering, "Cross at the corner!" And her old, little-kid face so happy when she's talking to Mickey Mouse. Mickey Mouse! Oh, geez, that's where she is! I'm getting radar from way across Brooklyn, from a bus traveling down Flatbush Avenue in the dark. There's almost no pedestrians. It's a dead city except for the streetlights, spreading that orange emptiness on every corner. The lit-up bus window has a smile-face pressed to the glass.

I make the corner by the bus stop in Olympic time. The B67 bus comes sliding up and I jump on, my lungs wheezing.

"Take it easy, son." The bus driver's like Walter, big and kind, except this guy's black. "I saw you. I wasn't going to leave without you."

I don't say it, but in this town most drivers would speed up when they saw you running for the bus. "Thanks, Mister," and I swing into the seat behind him.

"Marsha," I'm praying, "don't let any weird, creepy guys bother you. Be there safe with Mickey Mouse."

The bus is shooting into the night like we're the astronauts. Only a few working-type people coming off and going on shifts. They're glad to be sitting down, holding their work clothes in plastic bags on their laps in front of them. One of the bags says,

"I ♡ Schillenberger's Clothing Store on Delancey St."

Near Methodist Hospital a smiling, large lady with nurse's shoes hoists herself on board. Reminds me of Margaret Mary. "Maybelle, how are you doing tonight?" driver greets her.

"If you are talking to my feet, 'Terrible.' If you are talking to the rest of me, 'Just fine.'"

Coming home late from paper collecting, I've looked up at the hospital windows and thought, "Is somebody dying there right now?" It would be good to have this lady for their nurse, if somebody had to be dying.

I've got nervous eyes. They're roaming everywhere, checking out stuff I don't even care about. I'm a watcher again. For a while there, with Margaret Mary and Walter, I stopped being one.

More tired guys get on the bus with their *Daily News*es. Driver gives them all the "How you doing?" line. But he means it, like Walter. You'd think he'd get sick of driving his whole life, to Fulton Street, turning around, and coming back. He ought to growl at his customers. You'd think Walter would hate all those tall, heavy pots in the back of the restaurant on Seventh Avenue. But he won't curse them. He'll scrub and scour them clean as he can.

What if it's too late? What if poor, dopey Marsha lets herself down off the bus at the wrong stop, in the middle of nowhere? Here she'll be getting off, smiling because she's going to meet Mickey Mouse, and one of these barracudas smells a meal. In the dark places, they're always swimming and waiting.

This dude, or maybe it's a couple of them, spot her, wink to say, "This is a piece of cake," and move in for the kill. Maybe they've got a candy bar; maybe they don't even need that. They just tell her they're taking her somewhere nice, pull her in a dirty alley between the stores . . . Marsha! You couldn't understand there are people like sharks!

Near Fulton Street I'm hanging out the door as the bus stops, praying. The riders jump off and scuttle away, leaving the streets empty again. I know there are people who say, "Wouldn't she be better off dead? Her poor mother and father would really be better off without her. They're never going to get to go to her graduation or wedding, or hold their grandchildren. What's the reason for her living?" But they don't know everything! Mrs. Polini loves Marsha, maybe more than if she was a regular kid.

Moon's looking over the Hanson Building. His face frowns at me, warning, "There's trouble in the streets. Bad things are happening down there." Hurry, you damn bus!

It swings into the Fulton Street Mall and stops, and I hit the ground running.

"Night," calls the driver. Don't have to push anybody aside; the shoppers are all gone. Never seen it like this. The lit-up store windows show off their blue suede pants boots, "College Casuals," and "Dressy Spring Patents." Bald models stick one hip forward, jiving the ladies that this sleazy purple or green or red dress can make them that skinny too.

135

But all the shoppers, families, mothers, teenagers, they're home in bed, dreaming about winning the Lotto.

Where is the phone store? Right beyond A&S in the same building. I can see the bright window from here. Not a soul in front. I was wrong, or it's too late. I'm looking in now. There's a phone like an airplane and a solid-gold phone, and a Miss Piggy phone. And there's yellow-red-and-black Mickey Mouse, saying "Hi!" with his white glove. There's also a sniffling, and a crying-talking, coming from the dark doorway.

"Marsha!" She's huddled down, rubbing her nose, which is dripping. I kneel down by her. "Marsha, what happened? Are you O.K.?"

She looks up at me and smiles a little. "Robert."

I put my arms around her. Then I help her up. "Tell me what happened, Marsha? Did anybody hurt you?"

"I tol' him I been a good girl. I tol' Mickey Mouse, 'Robert is crying.' Mickey Mouse wouldn't talk to Marsha." She starts sniffling again.

"Hey, Marsha, it's bedtime. Mickey wants to rest, too. All day he has to wave to people, and he gets tired. You have to let him have a rest. Come on, I'm taking you home, hon'."

The same driver slaps open the doors on his bus. I boost Marsha in, and find I don't have the cash to pay our fares.

The driver says, "What's the matter, son?"

"Well, this is my friend from next door. She got

lost. Came downtown to see Mickey Mouse at the Phone Store. And I found her and I've got to bring her home."

He looks at Marsha. "Forget about the fare. Just sit right down and I'll have you home before you can say 'Jackie Robinson.' In fact, twenty-eight minutes, if you live near St. Saviour's."

She seems O.K. except for some dirt smudges and drips from her nose, which I pat away with an old Kleenex. She puts her head on my shoulder, and bingo, she's asleep. Thoughts I don't want come slithering around in my brain. There's a terrible tiredness, now that I'm not running anymore.

Maybe I'll just get back up in that tree and stay there—be a tree. Winters I could freeze over. Summers, feeling the green coming, going toward the sky. Peaceful life, no bad dreams. Winters and summers, years and years, watching the poor suckers down there. Dog walkers, and a sad hot-dog man. No good. Dawn Marie would come walking by and I'd unfreeze, stop being a tree, and start hurting again.

The bus is sliding up to our stop. I gently lift Marsha's head off me. "Come on, Marsha, your mom is waiting for you."

"Ma, Ma," she whimpers.

"I sure hope your friend is all right," the driver says.

"Yeah, thanks a lot. Good night."

Wish I was the Invisible Man. I need to get Marsha home without anybody seeing me. You can't

137

slink down a street with Marsha. Geez, with all the crimes I committed today, they're liable to think *I* kidnaped her.

The flat face of Marsha's house is asleep, eyelids down, door-mouth shut tight. No, wait, there's a light behind the tan shades in the living room.

"We're home now, Marsha. Sit down here on your step. That's right." She wants to tell somebody how bad it was, but she can't. The few words she had are scared away.

I tap on the door, then beat it into the bushes next to the steps. Mr. Polini is running down the hall. He fumbles and rattles it, trying to get the door open. I guess his hands are shaking. When he opens the door, his face is terrible. Those masks they always have on school auditorium curtains, one is smiling, one is weeping. He's got the weeping mask on.

He never said much. Mrs. Polini would be fussing with Marsha, and he'd just be there. You wouldn't know what he was thinking. Did he really like Marsha or not? It's all out on his face now. Tears of joy are spilling out of his eyes, but his mouth is curled way down. That must be how his life is: terrible pain that Marsha's the way she is, but still, she's his child.

"Edna, come!"

Mrs. Polini shuffles up behind him. If Marsha looks bad, Mrs. Polini looks as if she's raised herself out of the grave. Her hair is wild around her face, which is blotted, running off the edges. Only her

138

eyes burn in the white. When she sees Marsha, she starts sobbing, "Thank you, my God. Thank you." They're helping each other inside and the door closes.

I'm thinking, "All right, Mrs. Polini's God! Where do *I* go now?!"

"Robert, is that you? Why don't you just come on home?" I come out of the bushes. Margaret Mary is on the Polinis' walk, smiling at me and weeping. Walter's standing next to her, bawling. I'd cry too, only I never cry, do I?

12

They won't let me explain. "It's over and forgotten," Margaret Mary says. Geez, my mother never let you forget if you spilled a drink of milk. Margaret Mary is fixing hot chocolate and smiling to beat the band.

"I took the six-pack," I say.

"Walter saw it was gone."

"I never had beer before. I guess I got drunk. Maybe that's what made me break all your little animals. I'm real sorry, Margaret Mary." I start digging my knuckles in my eyes and sniveling like a five-year-old.

She runs over and starts patting my shoulder. "Never you mind. Never you mind." Then she reaches out and touches my cheek. "They're just plaster dolls, and they can't feel a thing. You just drink up your hot chocolate, and then you go get comfy in your own bed."

"The window at the rink, Walter. It was me threw the rock into it."

"We figured as how it was."

"I didn't mean it when I said you were a crazy ol' lady."

"Remember." She winks. "You said crazy, *nice* ol' lady. Even Walter thinks I'm crazy sometimes, don't you, Walter?"

"Sure do," he says real fast to help me out. Then he realizes what he's gotten into and tries to back up. "Oh, no, now, honey! I never said any such thing!"

"But you've thought it, now, haven't you?" For some reason, we all break up, laughing and laughing so hard.

Heather-Belle raises her head up off her quilt. "Doesn't she look like the dog in the commercials, moves its mouth and asks for Beefy-Time?" Walter slaps his knee.

Margaret Mary says, "Heather's telling us, 'There's a time to sleep and a time to go walking around looking for snacks.' This is the sleeping time." And we're off again, laughing like fools.

They shoo me up the stairs to bed. I turn at the top. The kitchen—I'd like a picture of it to put in my wallet, when I get a wallet, that is. There'd be Margaret Mary in it, glasses smiling up at the camera. And Walter, reading who won the Lotto in the

Daily News, happy for the guy, hoping it will be him someday. Big Boy's tail would be just going off the picture, and Heather would be grinning at the bottom. I can keep it always.

I'm sinking into bed. Good night, kind, good Margaret Mary. Good night sweet ol' Walter. Their voices come floating up through the register.

"Tomorrow we're going down together to that police station and find out how to adopt that boy. If Robert wants it, that is. And if there's lawyer reasons that say we can't, we'll just get a license, or whatever paper you need, to be his foster parents!"

They don't know the law always says you can't do something. But they want me, they really want me! They're not throwing me away! Maybe there *might* be a judge somewhere who has some sense, and he'd say, "Here's a kid without any real parents, and here's these parents without a kid. Let's get them together!"

I'm out of it till ten the next morning. Swimming up from deep-sleep places, I break into the light. Margaret Mary's standing in the door.

"Breakfast is ready, Robert," she says.

I almost break my neck getting down the stairs after her, I'm in such a hurry. Oatmeal is steaming in my bowl. Trickle the milk on it, pile on the sugar. "This stuff is *good!*"

"You ought to have seen us tucking into our oats, me and my sister and brothers. They didn't have the Captain this and Ka-bam that, like they do today."

"What were their names, your brothers and sister?"

"There was Thomas Harry, after my father. John William, Sarah-Jane Elizabeth—my mother liked to put a little frill to it—and George Henry, after her father. These days people don't name their babies after their folks anymore. Well, I can't exactly blame 'em. Some of my way-back relations looked pretty fierce with their beards and corsets. Would you like to see some of them? I've got a shoebox full over here." She's getting them out of the cupboard already, but I really do want to see them.

Margaret Mary feels so good, she can't stop talking. "Now, this is George Henry when he was a baby. Oh, my Lord! That's *me*! You don't want to see that!" She's hiding the picture against her.

"Please, can't I see it, Margaret Mary?"

She shows me this little girl in a white, short nightgown, with those little strap shoes on her chubby feet. She's holding her little arms up as if she wanted you to take her.

"You were cute," I tell Margaret Mary.

"No, I'll show you someone who was *really* cute. With the yellow hair, that's Sarah-Jane Elizabeth, Mamma's pride and worry. Oh, she loved us all, of course, but Sarah-Jane Elizabeth was littler and weaker. Frail, they used to say. And I was just so plain and healthy! More like my brothers, you know. I'd go to the park and try to play in all their games."

"Where are the fierce ones?"

"I guess Great-Uncle Andrew would get the vote.

143

That red beard could scare a baby into fits."

We're looking at a man under a round derby hat. His eyes and nose are all you can see sticking out of the beard. "Looks like he bites," I say.

Can't put it off any longer. I've got to face the garden. "Gee, I'd like to see the rest of these snapshots, but I'd better get to cleaning up outside. What I wrecked, you know."

"Oh, sure. You can see these anytime. They're always right here in the cupboard."

I step down slowly off the porch. Snow White and five dwarfs are still alive, and a speckled deer, and the pink stuck-up bird (wish I'd gotten him instead). But Thumper, and two little squirrels that always played together, they're just smashed into nothing. I pick up a few of the pieces, hoping I could mend them with glue. But that would be worse. The cracks would always remind me of what I did. Nope. I've got to buy new animals, and an elf on a mushroom, and Sneezy and Doc, for Margaret Mary. I don't care how many thousands of newspapers I have to sell. Also, the window at Roller Paradise. I can use all my money for that now, 'cause I won't be taking Dawn Marie to the city or anywhere.

The gate is actually singing on its hinge. I look up. It's Dawn Marie! She must know; everybody in the whole neighborhood must know. And she's a very religious person. How can she even look at a drunk like me, a curser and a wrecking wildman too?

"Robert, can I talk to you? I heard you brought

Marsha home last night. And I wanted to tell you . . . "
She's twisting that little heart locket she wears. "I
mean, *some* people wouldn't even want to bother
that much for a retarded person."

"Yeah, well, I just happened to think, you know,
with Mickey Mouse at the Phone Store, that's where
she'd go."

"She took a token out of the bowl in the kitchen.
That's how she got there. Robert, after what my
mother said, you didn't have to do anything for
anybody around here." She's almost crying. "It's
awful, but she just can't help saying things like that!"

"Oh, geez! It's all right, Dawn Marie. It's all right!"
Anything would be all right! You could kill me and
throw me in the Gowanus Canal if Dawn Marie
would only talk to me. I didn't think she ever would
again. "Please! Just forget it. I already did."

She's looking around at the mess. "You must have
felt pretty upset, I mean yesterday. But I knew you'd
never hurt anybody."

"I'm going to buy Margaret Mary a whole bunch
of new stuff, anything she wants."

"There's a garden store over on 9th Street where
they sell ducks and elves, swans even. Do you think
Margaret Mary would like a swan?"

"She didn't have one before, but maybe she would.
I could build a fake pond for it out of an old mirror,
or paint blue water on the concrete."

"Frogs, you could have frogs in the pond too."

"Say, would you like to go for a walk? Or, no, I
guess you couldn't, on account of your mother."

145

"Robert, you're my friend. My grandmother told me there was a saying in her town: 'True friends are like rubies—hard to find, but they last forever.' " I'm thinking I'm more like the ugly-rock or lump-of-coal type than a ruby. Then she says, "Robert, I told my mother I'm not going to stop being your friend, and I *would* like to go for a walk."

"Just let me tell Margaret Mary I'll clean up when I get back. Wait right there!" Whoops! I almost take a header over Heather-Belle. She heard "go for a walk." "Sorry, Heather! I'll take you for a walk next time. I promise!"

Margaret Mary's rocking and reading a second-hand *National Geographic* about Scotland: "Sturdy Folk, Honest Porridge." "There are some things," she says, "that can't wait and some that can. I'd say the garden will be here when you get back."

"Don't let Walter do any of it, will you? That's *my* job, and if if he was going to come home and pick up a broom or anything, I wouldn't go."

Margaret Mary swears she won't let Walter near the garden when he comes home from the restaurant, except to get down the walk and into the house.

We walk along, keeping about a foot and a half apart. It's Saturday, so she's not wearing her uniform. She's got on this blouse with little purple and green and yellow flowers around the neck, and puffy sleeves. And a pink, open sweater because it's not spring for sure yet.

"Your blouse matches those flowers." I point to

146

some that just jumped out of the dirt a minute before we came.

"It's so fast, isn't it?" she says. "I mean, the crocuses weren't there, and then they are."

"It really is." I'm watching her sideways. She has the same colors as spring, pink sweater, green and purple flowers on her blouse.

"Would you like to see something very interesting? I mean, I don't know if you're interested in things like that, but—"

"Oh, I am!"

"Most people wouldn't know they were there, it's so high up." She walks faster, sort of excited because she wants me to see this. We're coming around the corner of 10th Street. "There it is!" She's pointing along the top of an old-style apartment house. Faces, carved out of brownstone. A lady who must be a queen or somebody very strong. A man who's maybe a wizard; he's got a hood and a big, wise nose. At the ends these little grinning guys, very ugly.

"They're neat. I never would have thought to look up there." Mostly, I guess, I walk around looking down at the sidewalk.

Dawn Marie is really glad I like the faces. We gaze up awhile; then she says, "We could go over to the park. It's getting so pretty now."

The park is fizzing with green, like a shook-up lime soda. In the bushes it's Bird City.

"Listen to those birds. They're going crazy."

"It sounds like lunchtime in the cafeteria at St.

147

Saviour's. Do you think they're telling each other things, like where's the best place to get good worms or whatever it is they eat?"

"Oh, they do! In this *National Geographic*—Margaret Mary gets them from the second-hand store—it tells how they signal to each other if there are enemies around. They can even tell what weather is coming. You know, I saw this article about crickets. They can actually give you the temperature. Just count the chirps in fourteen—or is it forty seconds? I forget. But you add this number to it, and you've got the temperature."

"I think they're smarter than we are in lots of ways, the animals and birds and insects."

"Oh, they are! I saw these pictures of birds building nests that you wouldn't believe! Then they do these dances to pick a husband. . . ." I shouldn't have started on that. Dancing, picking a husband, Douglas. Oh, geez!

We're sitting on a bench. Her head is down and her hands are pressed together in her lap. "I'm going to the June Frolic with Douglas. My mother would be too upset if I didn't. He's a friend of the family, you know, and she's having this expensive dress made. But I've thought about it and thought about it, what I could do. It's this: I would be dancing with him, but I wouldn't have to be thinking about him. I could be thinking about someone else."

My heart flips over. Didn't I dream about this, or was it when I was drunk? She and I were in Paris, France, and it's all right for her to dance with other guys because she's looking at *me* over their shoulders!

Her finger is tracing these things kids scrawl on benches and walls and everywhere. TERRY LOVES DEE-DEE 4EVER, TYRONE THE BEST, ROBERT AND DAWN MARIE 4EVER. My face gets red-hot. Out of all the benches, we had to pick this one. She looks up; her eyes are bigger and more velvety looking at me. We don't even have to say anything.

We stand and start walking again, toward the plaza at the end of Prospect Park West. It's like Paris in *National Geographic*, with the horses on top of the arch, pawing up into the sky. Something is touching my hand, very shyly. Dawn Marie is slipping her fingers in mine. My chest is going to burst—oh, God, or somebody, Brooklyn's so beautiful!